An African Orphan

A Search For Meaning

Tobias Mwandala

Published by *T Counseling*

www.tcounseling.com

Calgary, Alberta, Canada

Copyright © 2014 by Tobias Mwandala

All rights reserved. No part of this publication may be reproduced, stored in a retrieval system or transmitted in any form or by any means, electronic, mechanical, photocopying, recording or any other, without the permission of the author and publisher. Any person(s) who does any unauthorized act may be liable to criminal prosecution and civil claims or damages.

Disclaimer

The story in this book is fiction. It is based on perspectives of the author only. The events, stories, places, names and descriptions in this book are used fictitiously—in no way these represent real life of people, names, places or things mentioned in this book.

For contribution or feedback, email the publisher at:
contact@tcounseling.com

Cover designer: Jenny Ryan
Edited by: Elise Mumert

Library and Archives Canada Cataloguing in Publication

Mwandala, Tobias, 1981-, author
    An African orphan : a search for meaning / Tobias Mwandala.

Issued in print and electronic formats.
ISBN 978-0-9936790-2-5 (pbk.).--ISBN 978-0-9936790-3-2 (kindle)

    I. Title.

PS8626.W36A65 2014   C813'.6   C2014-901842-8
                                                                               C2014-901843-6

Printed and bound in the United States of America

Published by T Counseling.
www.tcounseling.com
Calgary, Alberta, Canada

Available in paperback and eBook through Amazon and other retailers

To all who encouraged me to write this book: Gloria, Nathan and Jim. I'm grateful. To Natasha, Angelina and Zack—thank you for your lessons.

About the Author

Tobias Mwandala is a Canadian writer and social worker. He obtained a Bachelor of Science in Psychology from the University of Prince Edward Island in Charlottetown, PEI. Tobias also has both a Bachelor and Master of Social Work from the University of Calgary, Alberta, where he currently resides.

He enjoys travelling, scenery, nature and meeting people from various backgrounds. He loves food and spending time with his family.

Prologue

This is a story of an African orphan, Felix, who loses his parents as a very young boy. He embarks on a long journey searching for meaning in his life. On his journey he seeks to find answers and discover what there is to live for? Is there hope to be found in his ancestry, his companions, or himself? Read the story to find out how or if Felix will find the answers he seeks, will he live… or love?

Tobias Mwandala

An African Orphan

He found light in the darkness

CHAPTER 1

THE love Felix resisted for years was finally in his sight. Felix's heart was pounding when he saw Veronica the second time at their secondary school.

What should I say? What should I say? he whispered to himself. He knew at this time she won his heart. He realized that they were meant to be together. Felix felt that Veronica was a loving, humble and beautiful woman who gave him a real meaning to marry her.

Veronica's pupils widened, and her breathing rate increased as soon she saw Felix for the first time in their primary school. She thought Felix was a handsome and kind person. For Veronica, her love for Felix had never faded but sprang up afresh, when she saw him again.

"Where have you been my love? I hope this time you have come for me," Veronica said, gasping.

Felix never imagined that he would fall in love with a woman—after all the hardships that he had gone through in his life, including the loss of his mother. Felix's story began decades before he was born.

****

Felix grew up in Sub-Saharan Africa. In the late 1960s, during Angola's war, Felix's middle-aged parents fled Angola. They settled in Botswana, months after Botswana's independence. Felix was born in 1971. Three and half years later, his father Pedro passed away. Felix spent almost all his life without his father. Felix loved his mother—Estella so much that he would do anything for her. Felix's father spent most of his time outside home, at a mine where he worked, while Felix's mother stayed home with Felix most of the time. Sadly, his mother also passed away when he was a young boy. Felix was left without parents at a very young age. But he survived.

According to Felix's parents' tradition, the father had to name his child and the mother could accept or reject the name. Mothers usually accepted their husband's choice. Naming children was a father's responsibility. It was Pedro's task to name Felix. In that tradition, *Felix* represented only him, and that name had to reflect his personal character and appearance. The name *Felix* was derived from Pedro's brother, who lived in Angola. Pedro thought his son resembled his brother with his abundance of dark hair and long somber face. For that reason, Pedro named his son *Felix*.

Pedro gave Felix his own last name, *Munga, to* symbolize Felix's family ancestors and remind Felix where he belonged. When he was grown, Felix would be expected to pass *Munga* on to his own children. He would carry on the family legacy and culture: respect for elders and care of others, a love of education and the remembrance of one's identity and background.

Felix had a middle name as well, which Pedro gave to him. His middle name was *Mukeza*, which meant: *I will come or return.* It was Pedro's family tradition that Felix carried a middle name. The middle name *Mukeza* was given to Felix when he was two years old. It was a common practice in that tradition to assign a middle name months or even years after a child's birth. Felix was to take courage from the meaning of his middle name, in times of hardships or when he felt lost. In such moments, Felix was expected by his family to remember his middle name. For example, when his mother died, while he was a young boy, Felix reflected many times after that: *I am Mukeza—I will return to normal, and this is who I am.* Felix's middle name was like a spare part for Felix. The middle name played an important role for Felix as an adult. He could use it when he felt he could not belong to the other two names.

Much later in his life in Zambia, Felix's friends and relatives had middle names with meanings, as well. Felix's friends used to ask him if he had a middle name. When he shared that he had the middle name, he was welcomed by them—as part of their social group. For this reason, his friends often invited Felix to play and participate in traditional gatherings together. Felix developed a strong sense of belonging, as a result.

From time to time, when Felix was a schoolboy, Estella taught Felix about his father. It was not easy for Estella to teach Felix about their cultural roots. She encouraged him to connect with her sister and brother in Zambia. They too left Angola in the late 1960s and settled in Zambia, in a little village called *Zambezi Village* close to the Angolan border.

****

Estella's social network in Botswana was very small. She did not know many people in Botswana except a few friends who also had escaped Angolan war. Estella and Pedro took refuge in a mining town in central area of Botswana. The town was developing rapidly at the time. Gold and other precious stones were discovered. There was a huge demand for labour in the mining industry. More employees were recruited every month. On the first Monday—the hiring day—job applicants queued up at the mining office. To work in the mines, a man had to be physically fit and have a grade-seven education. Jobs were given on a first-come, first-served basis. Women were only allowed to apply for secretarial jobs like typing and bookkeeping. But Pedro did not allow Estella to work there. Pedro was a private and traditional person.

Pedro and Estella missed their native country, Angola and their extended-family members. They never thought they would leave Angola, its culture, traditions and food. But, they had to, in order to survive the war and to have a better future for themselves and their child. Although everything was foreign for Pedro in the beginning of his life in Botswana, he liked the country because it provided him peace. Estella also was glad to be in the new country because of its peacefulness. She also felt that the people in Botswana were accommodative and jovial. Both Pedro and Estella felt a sense of stability in their lives. Pedro started working as a miner, a job he wanted at the time. Estella spent most of her time at home caring for her son, Felix.

Tobias Mwandala

CHAPTER 2

PEDRO knew of the many job opportunities available in the mining industry. He also knew that he met all the requirements of becoming a miner. He went to apply for the job at the mining Human Resources office, twelve kilometers away from the house where he and Estella lived. There was no public transportation infrastructure in the town, and Pedro did not have a vehicle. So he had to walk everywhere. At 3:00 A.M., Pedro left home and walked to the Human Resources office. He arrived there around 5:00 A.M and lined up with others who had arrived at the office before him. There were 21 people in front of him in the line. That day the employer hired only 15 people, all of whom were ahead of Pedro on the queue. The hiring manager told Pedro and the rest to go back to their homes and return on the following month, during hiring day, first Monday of the month.

So the next month, Pedro woke up at 2:00 A.M. and walked to the hiring office. He arrived at the office one hour earlier than he had last time. In the queue, there were only six people ahead of him. Luckily, this time the mining company hired the first ten people who were on the line, including Pedro. As soon as he was hired, Pedro smiled, shook his waist, jumped and shouted, *"Yes"* to himself. Upon hiring, Pedro presented his national identification card and grade-seven education certificate, and signed a contract. The job gave Pedro a guaranteed monthly income of four hundred and fifty *pula*, Botswana's currency. Other benefits for Pedro included a two-bedroom townhouse located in the mining residential compound and company transportation from the compound to and from the mine.

Every day Pedro hurried to be on the minibus. The bus picked up miners from a designated station, which was about five-minutes' walk from Pedro's house. The houses in the mining residential compound were identical. They were all painted gray. It was a company offense for miners to paint the houses a different colour.

****

In Felix's later life, after Felix's father died, the uniform look of the houses prompted Felix to question why houses looked that way. When Felix was five years old he asked his mother, "Why they have to look the same?"

"To maintain and promote harmony and peace among miners," she responded.

She added, "If one miner's house looked different or a little better than another miner's house, people would talk. That could cause trouble in people's minds and in the underground mine. These are the things I didn't want your dad to feel when he was working under the earth. To work in the mine, a miner has to be peaceful with himself and others. A miner should not go to dig minerals in the underground with unstable emotions, because these emotions could cause the earth to shake."

She stroked Felix's hair and went on: "Pedro knew all this. He had to be in good spirits when he worked in the mine, so he didn't disturb the spirits and the dead of the underground. He respected them. Your father understood it was important not to carry bad feelings and thoughts into the ground. His coworkers had to do the same—freeing themselves from bad spirits, before going to work. Some miners have been killed and buried by the underground-mine accidents. It is usually hard to find the bodies of the deceased there. The spirits of the dead miners killed in these accidents roam around in the ground. These spirits should be respected."

"I wish your father were here to explain this to you. He prayed before he went to the mine, everyday. That gave him peace to carry with him. Remember, Felix, that just like your daddy, you have God. You cannot do all things by yourself," Estella cautioned her little son.

"Mother, did daddy die in the mine?" Felix asked, leaning his shoulder towards his mother.

"Yes. The mine collapsed when he was underground. But it wasn't because he was not a good person. He prayed everyday and knew the dangers that were involved in the mine. He is at peace now—in heaven," Estella answered instantly, squeezing Felix's right biceps towards her.

"I don't want to work in the mine. I'm scared of the dark and the spirits," Felix's little voice quavered.

"Don't worry Felix. The miners have torches that light up the dark places. And if you are good to the spirits, you don't have to worry about them. They wouldn't attack or do bad things to you. What happened to your father is sad—but accidents can happen anywhere in life," Estella assured Felix.

****

Every house had one redbrick chimney mounted on the roof. Each house in the mining residential compound had three windows: a large window for the living room, a medium window in the main bedroom, and a small one in the bathroom. There were two entrance doors to the houses: the kitchen door and the living-room door. The families living in these houses used the kitchen door as the main entrance. On some occasions, a family in the house allowed special visitors like priests to enter the house through the living-room door, to show the family's great respect and reverence for the church.

The compound was just twelve kilometers away from the mine, where Pedro worked before he died. Compound residents heard loud alarms coming from the mine. These daily alarms were used to signal the beginning and end of the miners' shifts. The same alarm was also used to warn miners about emergencies such as fires, underground mechanical failures and tunnel collapses. These alarms rang throughout the week, whether Pedro worked or not.

Pedro was a quiet man, with a well-built body and fairly tall height. He dressed in white casual shirts, brown trousers and sandals almost every day, except on Sundays, when he dressed in a simple *safari suit* (a pair of shiny black shoes, brown socks, khaki trousers and short-sleeved khaki shirt). He was not a very outgoing person. It was hard for the other mining families to guess what he liked and what activities he did for pleasure. But Pedro lived a rich inner life.

Though he did not talk politics with anyone, Pedro read newspapers and listened to the radio every morning. Pedro did not even go to bars or restaurants. In Pedro's local community in Botswana, it was not common to go out to eat or drink; instead, that was done in homes. For example, people would gather at one relative's house to eat food, drink wine, dance, sing and celebrate special occasions like birthdays. Nonetheless, Pedro did not even like to go to other people's places to enjoy himself. He preferred to spend such celebrations quietly at home.

Before Pedro died, he did not work on most Sundays. Instead, he attended church services. On one Sunday, as Pedro was walking to his church he felt something hit him on the face. When he looked around, holding his stinging cheek, he saw a white teenage boy with a football ball. The boy was playing football on the streets of another mining residential complex, where the mine managers lived.

Mostly white employees lived in this street. This residential complex had four-bedroom houses and the walls were made of small red bricks. The complex had essential facilities very close to it, including grocery stores, bakeries, butcher shops, medical clinics, and schools. The streets had towering trees planted between the street lanes, and the yards of these houses were bigger and cleaner than Pedro and

Estella's yard beside their little house.

Perhaps Pedro did not react angrily to the white boy who hit him in the face with his ball because of this calmness in his nature. For Pedro, the incident was an opportunity for him to teach the boy. Pedro liked to counsel young people.

"You see the white smoke up the hill there?" Pedro asked, pointing to the smoke at the mine.

"I know it. That's where my dad works," the boy answered, shaking his head up and down.

"I work there too, underground. There I dig minerals," said Pedro.

He added: "I might know your father. I believe he works on the main floor of the company; and he helps us out with paperwork."

"What's your name?" Pedro asked, opening his right hand.

"Jack; my name is Jack Philips," the boy answered, placing his right foot on the football ball.

"Yes, I work with your dad, and his name is Michael Philips, right?" Pedro said, calmly.

"Yes, that's right," Jack responded quickly.

While playing with his ball, Jack asked, "Do you know how to play football?"

"I used to when I was your age, but I don't anymore. Now I'm busy all the time," Pedro sighed.

"You can play with my son when he grows up, if you like," he added. "He is only an infant now," he explained further while he was looking down at Jack.

Jack nodded his head and looked up at Pedro's face, sporadically, while he played slowly with the ball within short parameters on the ground.

"Do you know what you want to be when you grow up?" Pedro asked, gazing at the boy.

"I want to play football in London," said Jack, while looking down at his ball.

"My dad is not home now, he went to South Africa on a business trip. He keeps telling me that I'm going to live with my grandparents in England, if I don't get good grades in school. There, I can play football; because my grandparents don't prevent me from doing things I like," Jack explained, clenching his teeth.

"I'm happy for you," said Pedro. "It's great that you have your grandparents who love you and want you to be yourself."

Jack chattered on: "Yes, I wish I was in Europe now. I don't like it here sometimes, because my dad tells me to do things I don't want to do. My friends from school do what they like, all the time. Most of my friends look like you."

"What do you mean?" Pedro asked.

"Your skin colour," with his right index finger, Jack reached out and touched Pedro's right hand.

"You mean most of your friends are Africans; black, yes?" Pedro said, nodding his head to Jack.

"Yes, yes," Jack said, nodding his head.

"Do you like them?" Pedro asked, looking at Jack.

"Yes, of course! They treat me right and we have fun. We play together. We sing together; and we dance together. My dad sometimes tells me not to spend so much time with my friends. He thinks I won't be good in school if I play with them all the time," Jack responded, confidently.

Pedro told Jack: "When I was a young boy like you in Angola, my father wanted me to be a soldier. But I didn't want to be that. So I studied hard in school. I spent most of my time reading books, so that my dad would think I couldn't be a good soldier.

Nonetheless, he never gave up pushing me to go off and fight. I did not become a soldier because my great-grandparents took me to live with them in their village. There I worked on my great-grandparents' farm, which I didn't like so much either. But I preferred being a farm worker to being a soldier. Then war broke out in Angola, and I regretted for not being a soldier; I would have fought for my country. My father passed away; a soldier killed him during a fight in Luanda, the capital city of Angola.

Sometimes, we cannot get all the things we want in life, but things usually work out the best. Things are the way they were meant to be. Perhaps if I continued to live in Angola during the war, I would have died by now. God brought me to Botswana and now, I have my own son, Felix. As well, may be my meeting with you was meant to happen."

"Don't you think so?" Pedro asked.

"Could be," Jack answered in a soft voice, scratching his head with his right hand.

"Don't worry my boy about life problems. Everyone experience them. These problems you are facing will go away. You are doing the right thing by talking about it and following your gut feelings," Pedro advised.

Jack replied, "I guess so; thank you sir. I'm going home now. My mom must be looking for me." Jack walked away from Pedro towards his house, kicking his ball in front of him.

Pedro smiled after talking with Jack. "May our Lord bless this boy," Pedro voiced while he walked in the street. He wished his son Felix were grown up and played with others, regardless of their social status.

After talking with Jack, Pedro continued on his way to his church. He was fifteen minutes late for the service. He did not worry about being late. He felt that he had done something important for Jack, something worth missing the beginning of the preacher's talk.

That day an Irish priest at the church preached about a sermon entitled: *"Being a good neighbour to others, regardless of visible differences."* After the sermon, the church choir sang songs both in English and *Tswana*, the local language. Pedro enjoyed sitting in the church pews and listening to the voices of the choir singers. The songs were rejuvenating. The voices from the choir were very sharp and loud, but soothing. When he listened to the songs, he forgot about his troubles in the mine, mine accidents and hard-physical labour.

The church congregation held members of both black and white racial backgrounds. Pedro was amazed that people at the church prayed together peacefully and respectfully, regardless of their skin colour. This was one of the reasons he liked to attend this church. Pedro's experiences of the Angolan war haunted his every moment. But he never admitted that in public or to Estella.

After the church service, some members gathered along the church verandas to greet each other, drink tea and eat biscuits prepared by the women in the church. Usually Pedro met with other men. He greeted them and listened to their conversations. The greetings involved long periods of handshakes and questions about one another's family. Pedro would ask his fellows what felt like endless questions. *How are you? Is your family well? Your wife in good health? How is your child? Your cousin?*

Pedro was a good listener, however. The men often talked about the progress of a variety of community church projects. One of the main projects involved clothing and food donations to the poor, as well as helping poor farmers by volunteering to weed crops and share knowledge about new farming methods. Pedro believed that without his spiritual faith and involvement in the church activities, he would not be a real human.

That day after church, Pedro told his friend, Kitso. "Without spirituality, a man is lost. We need to help others who have nothing. I mean nothing at all," Pedro clarified.

"Well, aren't we all doing what we can? But I wish the government would follow our footsteps—bringing people together as in our church," Kitso answered back, standing and lowering his eyebrows.

"I know many people don't want to talk about the elephant in the room, but I must say: we need to help our fellow Africans who are in poverty and struggling to gain freedom, as well. The priest wants us to take this route. We cannot sit down and listen to someone preach about good brotherhood and the need to help our neighbours without acting on these principles," Kitso finished.

"I agree. We have a long way to go. There's still hope though. There's hope!" Pedro responded softly, standing with his both hands in his trousers' pockets.

Pedro discussed: "Today, when I was walking in a rich neighbourhood, I met a young white boy namely—Jack—who talked to me with respect and dignity. He sought advice from me. We shared stories together. I was happy to see the spirit of *togetherness* in

Jack. I'm hopeful that our younger generation would make this world a better place, in which all of us would work together, play together and live together in peace and harmony, regardless of our visible differences."

"Amen. Have a good day my brother," said Kitso, raising his hands up.

"Thank you. You too my brother!" smiled Pedro.

****

"People have similar needs: to pursue dreams and have a better life," Pedro told Estella that night, after attending his church service.

"How so?" Estella asked.

Pedro explained: "On my way to church, I met a white boy by the name of Jack—who told me that he wanted to be a footballer in England. He was passionate about his dreams. I felt like he was my son. I also sensed that he treated me like I was his grandpa, with respect, and it didn't matter that I was a stranger to him. So, I advised him to follow his dreams. I'm sure he liked my advice and took it."

"That's good for you—Pedro," Estella reassured him.

"I did what was necessary to the boy and our Lord. We need more people like Jack in this world," Pedro said.

****

The following day, Pedro was scheduled to start his work shift at five o'clock in the morning at the mine. Pedro lived very close to the mine. The bus station, where the company bus picked him up to go to the mine, was less than a kilometer away from his house. He used to wake up one hour before his work shift commenced. That allowed Pedro time to put on his working clothes (a grey mining suit, heavy black boots and white protector cap with a torch on it) and to pack some food to eat during his lunch break.

On a working day, the mining company gave each miner a three hundred-millilitres bottle of milk and a bun to consume during the break. This was not enough food to sustain Pedro's energy for a grueling an eight-hour shift. But the bottle of milk he drank, thinking that this helped to strengthen his bones, and every little bit helped.

Products such as milk and bread were scarce in the country at the time. Some days Pedro would not consume the bun and milk that the company gave him; instead, he took those gifts home to the toddler Felix. Estella helped Felix drink the milk and broke the bun into small bits for Felix to place into his mouth. Felix looked forward to these treats.

Every time Felix heard their house door squeaking, he knew that it was his father returning. This would make Felix smile and squeak happily as well.

Pedro did not spend much time in caring for Felix physically, mentally and emotionally. Felix was a *mama's boy*. When Felix was two years old, on occasional afternoons, after Pedro came from work, Pedro asked Estella to bring Felix to him, and Felix would sit on Pedro's lap. Pedro would tickle Felix and whisper in his ears:

"Be a good boy to your mother."

"Are you a good boy?"

"Be who you want to be. I know that you can

achieve anything you want to become."

It was during these times that Pedro whispered his love for his little son into Felix's ears.

"When you grow up, take care of your mother. Bring money to her; buy a vehicle and nice clothes and jewelry. Take her places; love her, because she loves you more than anything in this world. And if I'm around, just remember to visit me. If you get married to a beautiful lady, don't let her forget your family," said Pedro.

Pedro would tickle Felix in his armpits, and both Pedro and Felix would roll with laughter. Sometimes, Pedro would tickle Felix so much that Felix would pee in his clothes and on Pedro's lap. Then, Pedro would give Felix back to Estella to clean and change his soiled clothes.

One day, Felix was playing while sitting on Pedro's lap under an avocado tree outside their house. Felix was too young to tell his dad that he wanted to use a toilet. Instead, Felix urinated on his father's laps. Pedro felt warm on his lap, suddenly. He jumped up and held out Felix with his hands and shouted: "Felix, why do you do this? Estella, Estella, come here! Felix is wet. He needs to be changed."

Estella was in the kitchen cooking food for supper (yellow sweet potatoes mixed groundnuts/peanuts) on a charcoal burner. When she heard Pedro shouting, she thought Felix was hurt. So she came running outside.

"Can't you just change him, isn't it just urine?" asked Estella.

Embarrassed, Pedro mumbled: "Well, I don't think it is just urine. Something smells. Besides, I have no time. I have to go to work. I need to change clothes and then eat and go. Could you please just change him," Pedro asked Estella and gave Felix to her.

"I always do this. When is there going to be a good time for you to change Felix? He is your son too, you know!" Estella frowned at Pedro.

Pedro looked down and went into the house to change his wet trousers.

Estella went in the kitchen and took the pot (with yellow sweet potatoes in it) and charcoal burner outside the house. She wanted to cook the food outside, because she felt the inside of the house was getting too hot. She also wanted to wash Felix's clothes, while she cooked. She placed extra water in the food and allowed it to simmer. Pedro relished this dish—yellow sweet potatoes mixed with groundnuts (peanuts). He always looked forward to that dish. He wanted to eat it before he left for work. The food was delicious, according to his taste.

Estella took out a basin from the bathroom, poured water in it and soaked Felix's soiled clothes. She scrubbed them with the same bar of soap that they used for bathing. It was a cloudy day and Estella was worried that it would rain that evening. When she was finished washing Felix's clothes, she hung them to dry on top of the kitchen chairs.

After an hour, the food was ready to be consumed. Estella poured the food into two bowls and placed them on the dining table in the kitchen. She filled two cups with water and placed them with spoons on the table. Pedro was in his bedroom, dressing up for his work. Estella called him: "*Father Felix* (meaning *the father of Felix*, a respectful way to call a man with a child in their culture), food is ready, please come and eat before you go to work."

Pedro answered: "I'm coming, just a minute, *Mama Felix* (meaning *the mother of Felix*, a respectful way to call a woman with a child in their culture)."

Before they started dining, Pedro told Estella: "It's December and raining already."

"It will probably stop. Rain in this month does not last long; wait until March. You better prepared with a good umbrella," Estella replied, gazing at Pedro.

"Where is my black umbrella?" asked Pedro, rolling his eyes.

"I don't know where you put it the last time when you used it. Check in the corner of the kitchen near the charcoal burner," said Estella.

"I can't find it," Pedro responded, while he continued to look for the umbrella.

"You can take mine, if you like; my red umbrella is in the bedroom wardrobe," Estella offered.

"No way! I'm not going to take your red umbrella to work. Red is not for miners. Besides, I work with a group of men. What would they think of me? They would think I have gone out of my mind or you have fed me *juju (black magic)*. It's not like I'm going to a market; I'm going to the mine. I won't take it. Please just help me to find my black umbrella," Pedro complained.

"It's just an umbrella. I don't think people mind. People mind their own businesses," Estella answered back.

"I wish people were like that. But, sorry: miners are not that way. They are men. They will notice that I'm carrying my wife's umbrella—a female umbrella," Pedro snorted.

He did not see the black umbrella—it was not

bright enough in the kitchen. It was dark outside, as well as in all the kitchen corners. The kitchen had one kerosene lamp. He carried the lamp as he walked around in the kitchen to look for the umbrella. Finally, Pedro found the black umbrella blended with the darkness in the kitchen corner, where Estella told him to look in the first place.

"I found it. Thank you," Pedro told Estella, and he started to eat the food.

"It looks like this is a heavy rain; it will last long, probably all night. I wish I was not scheduled to work today," Pedro mumbled through a mouthful. "Such times are good just to be with my family, drink tea and read my newspaper."

"We need money, and work is good for you," Estella advised Pedro, spooning more sweet potatoes into his bowl. He rolled his eyes.

The heavy rain continued pouring. Felix heard it splash heavily on the house. Outside, small streams were flowing from the front yard to the back yard of the house. The water was dirty and brown, mixed with the soil on the ground. The streams were full of leaves and other litter. Raindrops were making noise on the roof of their house, as if someone was throwing dozens of stones at them. It was icy rain.

Felix started to cry. Estella comforted him. She took him to their bedroom, placed him on their bed, and covered him with a blanket and told him: "Nothing will hurt you. I'm here. This is just noise from the rain. It will stop soon."

The house did not have tap water everyday. Sometimes, the tap would produce water for a day or two; on other days the family would not receive the water for a week or even months. When that happened, Estella and Pedro had to fetch for water from somewhere else—sometimes near, sometimes far. Fetching water was usually Estella's responsibility. So the rainfall on this day was an opportunity for Estella to collect some water from the rain.

Estella stepped outside the house and placed three empty buckets on the ground under the eaves, so that rainwater would flow down off the roof and into them. She was not wearing a raincoat and she did not bring her umbrella outside; so, she got wet and her clothes became soaked with raindrops. She did not mind to be soaked by the rain for few minutes outside, as it was a necessary routine and an amusement event for her. She felt cool from being wet by the rain.

Estella left the buckets to collect the water overnight. She hoped that it rained continuously through the night, although rain did not last long.

Pedro left the house with his umbrella. While he was outside walking and jumping over potholes of rainwater, his umbrella broke. The umbrella could no longer expand and stand automatically; he had to hold it in place on top of its metal rod to make it hold its shape. His work suit was soaked below his waistline from water on the ground splashing him as he walked to his company bus station. He could not see where he was going. There was no sun. There were no lights in the streets. He used his big company torch to light his path. He arrived at the station at the same time as the company bus. Pedro and five other miners who had been waiting already for the bus climbed aboard.

"Good day, my brothers!" The bus driver hollered from his seat.

"Yes, good day," Pedro responded along with the

other passengers as he took a seat.

"Ready to work?" the driver asked, smiling at everyone.

"Yes," everyone answered.

"It's raining heavily today," commented the man who was sitting next to Pedro. The man was wearing his mine suit and he appeared chubby and shorter than Pedro.

"Oh yes, this rain broke my umbrella and soaked my suit, as you can see," Pedro spoke, wrinkling his forehead and holding the umbrella upside down.

"You know, time goes fast in this type of weather. You won't notice that you have worked today. We will be back from work, before you know it," the man assured Pedro.

The man extended his right hand to Pedro and said: "I am Mr. Dig. One day, my superintendent called me '*Mr. Dig*,' and the name has stuck with me. Everyone at the mine and even my neighbours now call me Mr. Dig. Except my wife and children," he laughed. "So, I am sort of a foreman for my colleagues at work; because for some reason my superintendent thinks that I dig more minerals than others, " Mr. Dig continued to chat as the bus pulled up to the entrance of the mine.

"That's great! I'm happy for you. I will see you around," said Pedro, as he left the bus for work.

"What a flamboyant person, Mr. Dig?" Pedro sighed to himself, as he walked to the mine.

Pedro did not want to befriend with Mr. Dig, and thus, Pedro did not look for Mr. Dig at the mine, as Pedro did not want to surround himself with showy people. He thought the conversation he had with Mr. Dig was garish, as well.

****

Pedro came back after his shift that day without his broken umbrella. He had left it at the mine, forgetting that he had an umbrella when he went to work. Luckily, it was not raining when he returned. It was early morning, and as he walked Pedro sang.

> *"What a beautiful day*
> *Beautiful day*
> *Everyone is sleeping*
> *Sleeping*
> *I will have a great day."*

Pedro could smell the wet ground as he walked. Roosters were waking up and making noises. The clouds toward the east in the sky were red, and the sun was about to rise. It was a promising clear day.

When he arrived home, he saw the buckets in the corridors were full of rainwater. There were many dead leaves and small branches scattered around the yard. Pedro took the buckets inside the kitchen. He entered the house and woke Estella up by calling: "I'm here. I'm home."

She stretched and sighed, "It's morning already?"

She got up and went outside. She saw that Pedro had taken the buckets inside the house, and yelled to him: "Thank you for taking the buckets inside. We are lucky today. We won't need to go far to look for water."

Estella retrieved her short broom from the kitchen and started sweeping the fallen leaves, branches and other litter in the yard. The ground was not too wet, already beginning to dry in the warm morning air. According to Estella, the partially wet ground was not as challenging to be swept as dry ground. On days when the ground was hot and dry, dust from sweeping was too much for Estella. It caused her to cough when she swept. In dry-season days (between April and November) she sprinkled used water on the ground before she swept, to dampen down the dust.

As she swept in the mornings, the neighbours were also sweeping their yards. On these occasions, Estella greeted her neighbours: "Good morning neighbours."

Women who knew Estella would respond: "Good morning *Mama Felix* (a respectful way to address a woman with a child in that era)."

Sometimes both Estella and her neighbours would stop sweeping and chat about their husbands.

At times, Estella and her neighbours would stop sweeping because of small sandstorms in the area. In this season, Estella did not like the sandstorms. She believed the sandstorms carried ghosts that killed or injured people. These are some of the beliefs she carried from her parents. In addition, Estella believed that the sandstorms represented unhappy spirits of people who died from unfair acts. For her, the sandstorms needed to be left alone; they were not supposed to be disturbed. Estella feared the sandstorms, especially after they killed a young boy who was playing with sandstorms in the streets from the neighbourhood, in the dry season before.

The boy was playing with the sandstorms by throwing food towards them. Like many other young people in the community, the boy believed that throwing food towards the sandstorms would make them stop. The sandstorms threw the boy from the streets to a metal fence of a house, and as a result the boy died. So every time Estella saw the storms, she went inside the house and did not come out until after the storms disappeared.

Estella finished sweeping and went in the kitchen to cook and prepare breakfast for the family. Felix liked to eat porridge made of cornmeal, sugar and milk. Pedro and Estella enjoyed breakfast with milky tea with sugar in it, and bread with butter and jam. As she was preparing the food, she discovered that she did not have enough sugar for the porridge. So she walked over to one of her next-door neighbours to ask for some sugar.

When Estella knocked the neighbour's house door, a ten-year-old girl namely *Sarah* opened the door wearing a blue-school-dress uniform. She was getting ready to go to her primary school.

"Is your mom inside?" Estella asked about Sarah's mom who she called *"Sister-Mama Sarah,"* a polite way to address her female colleague who has children.

"Yes, she is here. What do you want?" Sarah replied.

"Well, I just came to borrow some sugar. My son likes to eat his porridge sweet, and I just realized that I don't have enough sugar while I was cooking the porridge," Estella explained.

The girl looked in the kitchen shelves and found her mother's pack of sugar. She took a cup and filled it with sugar and gave it to Estella: "Here is the sugar; just bring the cup whenever," Sarah said, standing on the kitchen doorstep.

"Thank you *my daughter* (Estella's respectful way of calling a female child). You are very kind. Tell your mother that I said hello," Estella told Sarah.

Estella returned to her house and poured the sugar into her own cup and washed the neighbour's cup. She placed it on the kitchen table so she couldn't forget to return it. Estella finished preparing breakfast and shouted for Pedro and Felix to come and eat breakfast. She fed Felix porridge before she started to eat her own bread.

Pedro took his time eating his breakfast. On that day, he was not scheduled to work a day shift. As soon as he finished eating the breakfast, he went to buy a local newspaper at a neighbourhood kiosk, which was five blocks away from his house. He enjoyed listening to the news on the radio and reading newspapers, especially in the mornings when he was not scheduled to work.

He walked to the kiosk with his radio turned on, listening to it keenly, and bought a newspaper. He bought bubble gum from the kiosk for himself, also.

"What's happening in the papers today?" Pedro asked the young boy who was working in the kiosk.

"Nothing really. We won the game." The boy was referring to the weekly news of a local football club that won a game against another town's team.

"That's great. Here is one *pula* (Botswana's money) for the newspaper and please give me five bubble gums. Keep the change," Pedro told the seller.

"Sir, you are not working today?" the boy asked, placing the money in his pocket.

"No, but I work tonight. It's good to take a break and know what's going on in the world," Pedro answered.

"Thank you. Have a good day sir," nodded the seller, accepting the change.

An African Orphan

Pedro went back to his house. As he walked to the house, he was chewing bubblegum, and was holding his newspaper with his left hand and the radio with his right hand. When he arrived at the house, he could not open the front door to enter inside the house. He called Estella to help him to open it.

Luckily, Estella was in the kitchen putting the breakfast dishes away. She heard Pedro coming and opened the door for him. As soon as Pedro entered, Estella told him to take care of Felix while she was away. She was going to a market to buy groceries.

Before she left for grocery shopping, she went to the neighbours to return the cup she borrowed from them. But nobody was home, so she left the cup at the neighbours in front of their door, and proceeded to the market. The market was not too far to walk. It was a half-hour-walking distance from Estella's home. Estella enjoyed going to the market. It was one of her ways to take a break from house chores.

Tobias Mwandala

CHAPTER 3

MANY months passed, Estella, Pedro and Felix continued to live their *normal* life. Felix was growing well. He did not have any known disease or health problems. At this time (1974), the three-year-old Felix was walking, running and talking, and Estella and Pedro felt happy about their child's development.

Pedro used to always say to his wife, "I have to kiss you before I go to work because I don't know if I will come back home. When I go to work, it's like going to church. You only go there to pray—nothing else. We don't chat or do anything petty when we are in the underground mine. When we come back from the underground, we pray to God: *thank you Lord for keeping us safe for our families."*

Although Pedro preferred to work in the mornings, his work shift changed constantly. Sometimes he was required to work in the evenings and nights. Most of the times, he worked at night and slept during the day.

On one Monday, he worked a night shift and returned home early morning around 7:00 A.M. Felix was asleep but Estella was awake. She heard Pedro open the door. The front door was made of aluminum. It was heavy and made squeaky noises every time it moved.

"It was a long hard night," Pedro complained.

"I'm doing it for my son. I want Felix to get an education and be a manager of a company; not like me!" Pedro uttered.

"I work long hours. This is a very hard job. We are not paid well. I do not want to see my son doing it. Yes, we are driven to work and back, and they gave us a house, but that is still not good enough for Felix," Pedro stated, while he grinded his teeth with frustration.

"Look at it this way: we left the war behind in Angola. We are not dead; we are here. We are not starving, and you have steady work. You have a beautiful son; and I am always here for you," said Estella. "Let me massage your feet."

"Sure, darling!" Pedro laughed.

****

Felix's parents had lived in a small village in northwestern area of Botswana, before they moved to work at the mines in the central area of Botswana. At the time, most people in the village were pastoral farmers. Estella and Pedro did not like farming, although their parents in Angola were very good subsistence farmers. Estella and Pedro wanted to work in a town or even a city. They believed living on a farm away from people would hamper them from being part of central government's job opportunities, which was a common belief among young people at the time. In the 1960s (the generation of Pedro and Estella), numerous social and political movements were taking place in the Sub-Sahara Africa. Africans were fighting for intellectual, political and social freedom.

In that time, Europeans (mostly colonialists) owned large private companies, commercial farms, and mines, social and political institutions in southern Africa. Africans were awakening and wanted to be free from colonial power. The majority of black Africans were not allowed to shop or mingle with white Africans/Europeans or be employed in high-ranking government positions. Those conditions minimized Pedro's chances of working in other companies but in the mine, where the owners mostly needed many labour workers.

Pedro and Estella did not have to participate in changing colonialism. They were not considered at the time as "freedom fighters." They were not revolutionaries either, but they wanted to have freedom, in order to have a better life. For them, that meant working in the government, having an access to modern schools, hospitals and innovations of the time.

Indeed, the conditions in the southern Africa impacted Felix's parents, and they wanted Felix to have a better life than they did. They wanted Felix to complete post-secondary education and have a high-ranking position in the government. For them, a government job was a respected job their son could have, and attending a post-secondary institution was something Pedro desired but never achieved in his time. Through listening to his radio and reading newspapers, Pedro became more aware of many African nations gaining independence at the time. As a result, he believed that his son would have the opportunity of receiving a post-secondary education in the future and achieve what his parents wished for him.

****

One Wednesday, during the rain season of 1974, Estella was chatting with Sister-Mama Sarah at her house, Estella's next-door neighbour. She had gone there with Felix tied to her back with a cloth—a common practice of carrying children for most mothers in that community. Felix was three and half years old.

"Sit down my *sister*," said Sister-Mama Sarah, spreading a mat on the ground. Estella undid her baby from her back and removed her footwear and then she, her baby and Sister-Mama Sarah all sat down on the mat.

They chatted for a while and gossiped about food, news in the neighbourhood and about whose kids in the neighbourhood weren't behaving.

Sister-Mama Sarah brought some juice and pancakes from her kitchen and said, "Estella, feed the baby, you know he is my child too, hey?"

"My sister! You know how to do it in style, eehh?" joked Estella, while feeding a pancake to Felix.

While they were still enjoying one another's company, Estella jerked up and asked, "What's that noise?"

"Look, I think somebody has got company,"

An African Orphan

answered Sister-Mama Sarah, with a serene giggle and pointing to Estella's yard.

Estella turned around and looked over the wood fence to her house: "He is wearing a miner's hat and a matching suit and he is knocking on my door!" complained Estella.

"Wait a minute, is he coming from the mine?" asked Sister-Mama Sarah.

Estella collapsed on the ground. Her eyes were wider with tears, "That definitely can't be good news, have you seen the grave look on that man's face?" asked Estella, still lying down on the ground shaking.

"Take it easy my sister (referring to Estella), the baby needs his mother to be sound and alive; besides how would you know? It could be good news," said Sister-Mama Sarah, pulling Estella by her arm and aiding her to her feet.

"Excuse me, I have to go and see what that man wants," said Estella, lifting her baby off the ground.

"Take it easy my sister, eh? I will be here if you need me," said Sister-Mama Sarah, securing Felix onto Estella's back.

"I hope it's good news; maybe they increased Pedro's salary," Sister-Mama Sarah gossiped.

"Let me go; we will talk later," Estella told Sister-Mama Sarah and walked back to her house.

"Can I help you?" Estella asked the man, her hands trembling.

"My name is Mr. Dig. I work with your husband. My superintendent has sent me. I'm sorry. I have bad news for you," Mr. Dig said, with his head lowered and his arms folded on his chest.

"Has something happened to Pedro?" moaned Estella loudly.

"I am afraid so," apologised Mr. Dig.

"What is it about my husband? Is he okay? Is he okay? Is he in the hospital? What happened to him?" Estella asked, trembling.

"Here is the letter from my boss," said Mr. Dig.

"Please just tell me what happened to my husband," Estella pleaded while wheezing.

"We cannot find him. The underground mine collapsed and only a few miners managed to get out of the tunnels. I'm afraid the rest may never come out. Madam, your husband is dead," Mr. Dig stated.

"I knew it, oh no! My Pedro, why have you done this to us?" moaned Estella, falling down on her knees.

Estella wailed and collapsed on the ground with Felix on her back. Sister-Mama Sarah and her daughter (Sarah) heard and saw Estella crying; they rushed to Estella's house and lifted her up from the ground. They took her into the house. Sarah took Felix to his bed.

"Father Felix, where are you?" Where have you gone? You have left a widow and a wonderful son behind! Come back! Come back!" Estella wailed.

Sister-Mama Sarah placed her arms on Estella's shoulder: "I am so sorry my sister. Gain heart my sister, gain heart," she said over and over again.

Within an hour, other neighbours started to gather into Estella's yard and joined in the wailing.

Mr. Dig held his mining cap under his right arm as he looked onto the crowd that was almost closing in a ring.

"Sorry I had to come by wearing this mining suit as I wanted to represent the mine when delivering the message," Mr. Dig explained to Estella.

Mr. Dig was that kind of a person who liked being in connection with power and authority; at least he wanted people to see him that way.

Mr. Dig bowed courteously and put on his hat and left the house.

Estella cried for hours. Her laments filled the spaces between her sobs. "God, what have you done to me? Why did you take my Pedro? He was still young. Why me? Why us? Can't you see we have a young child? What am I going to tell Felix about his father? Oh God, help me! Pedro!"

Estella tied a black cloth around the sides of her head, a sign of respect for her deceased husband. According to Estella's tribal culture from Angola, few hours after receiving the news of Pedro's death, Estella, as a wife of the deceased, she had to dress with a black cloth tied around the sides of her head for at least one year after her husband's death. Within that year, she would not be supposed to engage in any romantic relationship with another man. This was one of her traditions to respect the deceased.

Within the same day of Pedro's passing, many people had gathered in Estella's yard.

While a couple of them joined in the moaning, others were busy asking Estella's next-door neighbour, Sister-Mama Sarah what had happened. Sister-Mama Sarah explained that Pedro died at the mine, buried down under the earth. Men from the neighbourhood started talking among one another and told others who knew Pedro to come to the funeral. The men brought firewood from their houses and started a fire pit at Estella's house. Some men came to the house with their chairs. Other men brought tents and placed them outside the house in the front yard—five meters above the ground, so as to shelter people (who were mourning at the house) from the January rain.

Women began moving Estella and Pedro's family items such as pictures, ornaments and clothes from the house's living room and kitchen into the bedroom to make way for people—mainly women—who came to mourn Pedro's passing. During this time, men stayed outside the house while women went in. About sixty people came to the house. Within forty-eight hours of receiving the news about Pedro's death, people arrived for the funeral from different homes in the mining compound where Pedro and his family were known. Some people knew Pedro from the neighbourhood; some knew Pedro from his church, and others knew him from the mine—all came to commemorate Pedro's life.

Some of the women brought big pots, pans and dishes to use at the house. Mr. Dig visited the house again with a company vehicle full of essential goods for the funeral. He brought two 25-kiligrams bags of rice; 20-litres container of cooking oil, one 10-kilograms of bag of beans; five 2-kilograms packages of sugar; twenty loaves of bread; a 10-kilograms of bag of onions; and another 10-kilograms bag of dry local small fish. Men outside the house helped Mr. Dig unload the foodstuffs from the vehicle.

Mr. Dig was sent by his company to assist Estella with Pedro's funeral costs. Mr. Dig called Estella into the house backyard and privately handed five hundred pula to her to use as she wished.

Estella looked at the money in Mr. Dig's hand and clapped her hands three times (a sign of thankfulness). "This is great help," said Estella,

"Thank you very much sir."

"You are welcome, I'm glad I can help," said Mr. Dig with a gentle smile on his face, "Pedro was like a brother to me."

The women cooked food at the funeral. They prepared three meals a day (breakfast, lunch and supper) for the people who came to the house. Some men went to a local tavern and brought twenty-five litres of local beer made from corn and yeast. Men drank in evenings. Some people came to the house only during the daytime. Others came only at night to sleep; and some people stayed all day and night at the funeral.

It was cultural practice that Pedro's family and friends spent the night at Estella's home to give company to the moaning family. Men slept outside the house in the tent. Women slept inside the house, mostly in the living room; they had brought blankets and bed sheets from their homes. It was cold at night. Nonetheless, two fire pits started by the men (one in front of the house and another in the back yard) warmed the night.

Later that night, Sister-Mama Sarah said to Estella: "Now almost everybody is here, unless you have other relatives in the country or abroad, that we have to sermon, let me know."

Estella was sobbing silently.

"Anyone you have here in Botswana or somewhere else? We can contact and inform them about Pedro's death, on your behalf," she offered to Estella.

"Other than you *sister*, and little Felix here, I don't have any relatives in Botswana," Estella replied, patting Sister-Mama Sarah's hand.

Estella told her neighbour: "I have relatives in Zambia and Angola and some of them may have moved from Angola to Congo, but I never had any close contact with any of my relatives except a few letters from one or two who live in Zambia."

"Who is in there? Do you have their address?" Sister-Mama Sarah inquired.

"My sister and brother are in there. I have their address; it's in my purse. I put it in the wardrobe in the bedroom there," Estella pointed.

Sister-Mama Sarah helped Estella write a letter to her brother and sister about Pedro. An appointed elder from Pedro's church came also and asked Estella about her relatives in Botswana. Again, she told the elder that she did not have any relatives except her brother and sister who lived in abroad.

"Is it all right to have the funeral this Friday?" the elder asked Estella. It was two days after Pedro's death.

Estella answered: "Yes, there is no need to wait. They could not find Pedro's body buried in the underground mine."

"We can lay to rest any personal items that Pedro left. What items do you think we can bury?" the elder asked.

"His mining uniform suit, and his shoes, watch and hat. I will keep his radio for Felix," Estella responded respectfully.

Her eyes filled up. She fell on the ground and started crying loudly: "Pedro, what have you done to me? What have you done to your son?"

Sister-Mama Sarah rushed to her and comforted her.

The elder blinked slowly and laid his hand on

Estella's shoulder. "Everything is dealt with. Don't worry about anything."

Sister-Mama Sarah took Estella inside the house, murmuring, "Everything will be alright."

Sitting Estella down at the kitchen table, Sister-Mama Sarah continued, "I'm going to mail the letter to your sister and brother in Zambia, letting them know about your husband passing."

"Sarah!" she ordered her daughter, "Please keep an eye on Sister-Mama Felix. I will be back shortly."

So Pedro's burial day was scheduled for Friday. Early Friday morning, the church elder came to Estella's house and took Pedro's belongings that were to be buried that afternoon.

Mr. Dig also came that morning and met with the elder. He introduced himself as a representative from Pedro's workplace; and the elder introduced himself to Mr. Dig as a representative from Pedro's church. Both men discussed arrangements for the burial. Mr. Dig brought a coffin paid for by his company, and the coffin was to be used to bury Pedro's belongings.

"All we have is Pedro's belongings. They couldn't find his body," the elder told Mr. Dig.

"I'm aware of that," Mr. Dig responded. Pedro's unknown whereabouts floated around them like a cloud.

The elder took the belongings and placed them in the coffin. Mr. Dig helped the elder haul the coffin into the company truck that Mr. Dig brought that morning. The elder filled Estella and Sister-Mama Sarah in about the arrangements for the day.

The elder told Estella to go to Pedro's church at 11:00 that morning to give respect to Pedro before the burial took place. After Estella was informed, all the people at the house were then told about the plans. Around 10:30 A.M., many people prepared themselves and went to the church. The closed coffin with Pedro's belongings was placed at the front of the church. The pastor at the church prayed over it and prayed with the people. The choir sang several of Pedro's favourite hymns.

> *"No one is perfect; we'll all pass; let's keep faith and love for one another."*

Estella was crying quietly. She stood side by side with Sister-Mama Sarah. She had not once left Estella's side. Felix was not brought to the church or the burial site. Sarah took care of Felix at home.

After the church service, the people went to the burial site that was located out in the bush, fifteen kilometers north from the mining compound. Pedro's company offered three trucks to be used for transporting people to and from the burial site. One of the trucks carried the coffin, Estella and Sister-Mama Sarah, Mr. Dig, the church elder and a few other church elders and company officials. The other two trucks carried as many people as could be fit into them, including church and company members and family friends. The people were singing songs as they rode along to the burial site. Anyone who couldn't fit into the vehicles walked behind the trucks from the house and the church to the burial site.

Eight of the most muscled men from Pedro's residential compound had arrived an hour earlier than the funeral guests. Mr. Dig had instructed these men to go and dig the site for Pedro's burial. Mr. Dig had offered them a ten-litres container of local beer and a one hundred pula for completing the job.

After everyone had arrived singing, the strong men placed Pedro's coffin into their hole, and started to shovel dirt back into it. Estella and few other women from her neighbourhood began crying again. Others sang songs while the burial took place. After the burial, people went home.

A few women had remained at the house to cook and prepare drinks for the mourners once they had returned from the burial. Around 2:30 P.M., people started arriving back at the house. The women prepared rice, chicken and beans for lunch. The women divided the mourners into groups (about eight people grouping in each) and gave food to all.

It was the end of Pedro's funeral rituals. After the people ate the food, they started to leave the house. Some told Estella to take care of herself. Some people gave addresses to Estella so she could contact them if she needed help. Some left without saying anything.

The following day, there were very few people at the house. After most mourners left the house, Sister-Mama Sarah and few other women started cleaning up both inside and outside the house. She also cooked food and made sure Estella and Felix ate the food that was prepared for them. She instructed her daughter, Sarah to take care of Felix at her house, while she performed those duties.

The eight strongmen helped Estella to remove the tents from the yard and cleaned up the fire pits. A couple of women from the neighbourhood helped with cleaning up dishes, taking them back to the houses where they belonged. They also swept the yard. Sister-Mama Sarah also reorganized Estella's personal items in the house.

Mr. Dig had told Estella to continue living in the house as long as she wanted. He assured Estella that the mining company would not take the house away from the family. Mr. Dig kept repeating the company's official policy: *"The house belongs to the deceased's next of kin."*

In the following year after Pedro's passing, Felix turned four years old. In that year, Estella received a letter from her sister Gertrude. It read:

"Dear Estella,

I am so sorry that your husband passed away. Ricardo and I both send our condolences to you and little Felix. We would be happy to help you in any way you wish. We are sorry that we cannot come to Botswana. We have heard that it would be difficult for us to pass through the border, as we don't currently have passports. We don't even have government identification cards here. Thinking about this now, we will apply for the documents. It takes a long time to receive them, but we will keep you in our prayers in the meantime.

I hope Felix is doing well. How old is he now? Sister, I miss you. I wish we could all be together in one place. This is difficult for us, and I'm sure for you as well. Do you know anyone from Angola there? It is peaceful here. As it is on the address I gave you, we live in small village called *Zambezi Village*. The village is easy to find because it is near the *boma*, a central town in northwestern Zambia. We pray that you bring Felix to us one day and we would love to see you both. We are both devastated that we did not have a chance to see Pedro one more time. Ricardo sends his special love.

May God bless you and Felix,

Gertrude.

Estella cried quietly as she read the letter. Tears dripped onto the paper.

Felix saw them and asked: "Mom, why are you crying?"

Estella told him: "Nothing bad, it is just that I miss your daddy."

****

With help from her neighbours and Pedro's company benefits, Estella continued to live in Botswana until Felix turned six years old. The six-year-old Felix did not ask his mother many questions about his dad. Estella started to feel lonely in Botswana and feared for Felix's social wellbeing. She wanted to be close with her own blood, her sister and brother.

Eventually, Estella felt that she had no choice but to leave Botswana. She wrote letters to Pedro's church and the mining company that she was leaving the country. The church collected some money for her, which she used for transportation from Botswana to Zambia.

In her letter to Pedro's old employers, she did not ask for money from the company; instead, she thanked the company for what they did for her family and told the company that she was leaving Botswana. The mining company never responded to her letters.

A day before leaving the country, she went with Felix to say her goodbyes to Sister-Mama Sarah.

"Sister-Mama Sarah, I have to leave this country so

that I can be with my brother and sister in Zambezi Village," Estella said.

"This is your country. We are your family, Sister-Mama Felix! We have survived all along together—you don't have to leave sister!" Sister-Mama Sarah cried.

"You have been very kind to me Sister-Mama Sarah, and I can never repay what you have given me all my time here in Botswana. Thank you and God bless you," Estella told Sister-Mama Sarah.

Estella was feeling sad and somewhat embarrassed at this point. She had tears coming from her eyes and she felt her throat closing up. She could only murmur her uncertain goodbyes to this wonderful woman.

Sister-Mama Sarah called: "Sarah, come outside and say goodbye to your aunt, Sister-Mama Felix and your young cousin, Felix."

Sarah came outside the house, with a book in her hands. She had been studying math inside the house. While holding her book in one hand, Sarah hugged Felix and Estella and said: "Felix goodbye. Have a nice trip auntie." Sarah looked on the ground with her eyes wet.

Sister-Mama Sarah placed her hand on Sarah's shoulder and told Estella: "Take care my sister."

Sister-Mama Sarah rushed inside her house and returned with a handmade sweater and blanket she had sewn and gave them to Estella and told her: "This is for you to keep. The blanket is for Felix and the sweater is for you Sister-Mama Felix, to keep yourselves warm. Zambia can be very cold, I hear. Don't forget Botswana and us. You can always come back. We will always be here for you when you come. Please visit."

CHAPTER 4

AFTER saying goodbyes to their neighbours, the following day, Estella and Felix took their luggage (Estella's small handbag and a large satchel with extra clothes for Felix and Estella, their family pictures and Pedro's radio) and began their journey to live with Gertrude and brother Ricardo in *Zambezi Village*. This was the farthest Estella and Felix had ever travelled.

Estella and Felix took a bus from central Botswana, where they used to live to a border town connected to four countries: Namibia, Zimbabwe, Zambia and Botswana. Estella and Felix arrived at the Botswana's side of the town. The town was very busy with people moving in every direction, crossing the different borders into the four countries.

There was a small market at the town where people sold souvenirs from all the four countries. Felix saw a postcard with a photo of an elephant and *Victoria Falls* on it. He liked the postcard. He asked his mother to buy it for him.

"Mom, can you buy me this card," Felix asked Estella, pointing to the elephant postcard.

"Yes, but only this one. Nothing else," she

warned.

"Ok!" said Felix, clapping his hands and smiling.

"Do you know that we are going there? That's Livingstone town in Zambia," she told Felix.

"Really? I like it. Thank you for taking me there," said Felix, while he hugged her.

"It's time to go now," Estella replied.

Before they took a ferry to cross the *Zambezi River* between Zambia and Botswana, they walked up to the Botswana-border officials, who were wearing civilian clothes.

Estella told them, "We are visiting Zambia. My brother and sister live there."

"Please show your identifications and give me your luggage, including your purse," the border officials ordered.

"Here is my Botswana national identification card and birth certificate for my son, Felix," she told them, and presented her documents and luggage.

The officials took Estella's documents and bags to the border office. They removed all the items from Estella's luggage and purse and examined everything. Then they told Estella she could go in the office and repack the items into the bags.

"So, how long will you be staying there?" the officials asked Estella while she packed.

"I'm not sure; but I should be back to my country soon," said Estella.

"I thought we weren't going back?" asked Felix.

Estella looked at Felix and shushed him, putting her finger against his mouth. She leaned down and told Felix, quietly: "Shee! Stop! We are coming back Felix."

"Okay go, come back soon to Botswana, and have

a nice stay in Zambia, Madam; after you cross the river, go over there to the Zambian border officials and present your papers again," the Botswana-border officials instructed.

Estella put on the bags and took Felix's hand, leading him quickly out of the office before he could say anything else.

Felix was excited to see the Zambezi River. "Mom, look, I see fish in the water. It must be deep. I can swim," Felix said.

"No, no, Felix! It's deep there. You cannot swim. It's not for swimming. Look at the river and see how the water is moving fast. It's dangerous," Estella cautioned as they climbed aboard.

Just few minutes later, Estella and Felix were in the Zambian part of the border town. At the Zambian border all the officials Estella and Felix met there wore military uniforms. Estella swallowed.

"What is your business here?" One border official asked.

"We are here to cross the border. I'm going to visit Zambia," Estella said.

"Why visit this country? Why not Namibia or Zimbabwe? Why here?" the official asked.

"Because we love Zambia so much. We cannot resist this place. That's why!" Estella smiled and told the official.

The official smiled back and told Estella to go. "Take care of your mother," he told Felix, who was clinging to Estella's hand peering up at him.

As they left the office, Estella prayed quietly to herself. *"Thank you Lord. We are here."*

Across the street there was a bus station. Estella and Felix crossed to it with their luggage. The station was crowded with people standing and walking with their bags. It was loud in the station: people were selling food, drinks, souvenirs and clothing. Bus conductors were selling bus tickets and calling people to go on their buses. A conductor for the bus going to Livingstone yelled to passengers: *"Livingstone, Livingstone, Livingstone bus is going now."* There were lineups of both people and buses for different destinations. Buses had names of their intended destinations: *"Livingstone," "Harare,"* and *"Windhoek."* There were also express buses to *"Gaborone"* and *"Pretoria."*

Before Estella and Felix boarded the bus to Livingstone, they went and sat on the bench of a food booth. Both of them were feeling tired but thrilled to be closer to their goal. Felix was breathing fast and wheezing as he sat on the bench. Estella was worried, though Felix had never shown signs of asthma before. She held Felix's hand and kept reassuring Felix, telling him to relax and breath slow.

Felix was not wearing comfortable shoes. They were a smaller size of second-hand *presidential* (school) closed-toed shoes that were given to him by Mr. Dig after Pedro's burial. The shoes had belonged to Mr. Dig's ten-year-old son, but the boy did not like the shoes any longer and he had grown out of them.

"Mom, my shoes are hurting me. They are too tight," Felix complained.

"Let me see your feet." Estella pulled Felix's shoes off his feet.

"Oh! Mom, it's aching," Felix screamed.

"Your shoes are too small for you. I'm sorry, I didn't see that. Let me buy you sandals here at the station so that you can walk well, and your feet won't ache. Right?" Estella asked.

"Okay," Felix sniffed.

Estella called a street vendor who was selling sandals and socks from a pushcart and asked him if he had size three sandals.

"Yes madam, I have lots here. Some are made in China; others are made locally here and some are from South Africa. I recommend the South African ones, they are cheap and made strong," the street vendor said, while sorting through his goods. The vendor himself was wearing sandals and beach clothes—a t-shirt and trousers made with thin cotton.

"How much are they?" Estella asked.

"Not that expensive: only five *kwacha* each, Zambian money, the vendor stated.

"I have three pula, Botswana's money. Can you accept this much?" Estella took the money from her purse and showed it to the vendor.

"Yes, I can accept that much," the vendor said.

He added: "Madam, I have socks as well. You might need them. They are good to have on the bus, especially at night when it's cold. You are from Botswana, right? I can tell, ha-ha-ha! Botswana is hot. Here can be very cold: It rains a lot too. We are very friendly people. There are many people from different tribes and languages living here. We all get along well. We have never had a civil war. So welcome to Zambia. You are in good soil." the vendor chatted as he took out a pair of sandals from the cart.

"Good to know. Thank you." Estella smiled. "Okay, I'll give you one pula for two pairs of socks, one kid's size and an adult size. How's that?" Estella asked.

"Agreed! You are very good mother to your son;

and you are very beautiful. For these reasons, you can take both pairs for one pula, you save one pula and I lose one pula. My welcome gift," said the vendor as he smiled.

"Thank you. You are a very kind man. Have a good day! We have to catch the bus now," said Estella. She took the socks and put them in her purse. The vendor walked away and disappeared in the crowd at the station.

Felix told his mother: "Mom, I'm hungry." So they bought mango juice, groundnuts (peanuts) and cassava from the booth there. They ate everything and drank the juice. Felix wanted to use a toilet, and so did Estella. The public toilets were well-maintained, but people had to pay money to access the toilets. There was a muscular and six-foot tall man who stood near the entrance doors collecting toilet fees from people before they could enter.

Estella and Felix paid a two-pula note to the man. Felix used the male washroom and Estella used the female washroom. After, Estella and Felix ran to the bus that was going to Livingstone. Estella could not run as fast as Felix. She was wearing sandals and a Botswana's traditional dress (yellow long dress with a length close to her feet). Felix was wearing his new sandals, a pair of blue shorts and a buttoned white short-sleeved shirt.

When they boarded the bus there were few passengers already in seats. The bus conductor asked Estella if he could put her luggage in the bus trunk, outside the bus. Estella refused and insisted to place her luggage in the bus cabins, close to her seat. She preferred to have their luggage in her sight. Before she left Botswana, Sister-Mama Sarah had advised

Estella to watch her luggage all the time during the trip.

Estella and Felix sat four seats away from the driver. The bus had a seating capacity of forty-four passengers, but it had fifty passengers on this occasion. Five passengers stood on the bus aisle. One passenger had to sit on the bus-engine cap between the driver and passenger seats.

While the bus was filling up with people, passengers were chatting with one another. A woman who sat across the aisle from Estella began telling her to put Felix on her lap instead of him occupying a bus seat.

She advised: "If he sits on your lap, then you won't need to pay the bus fare for him. But don't put him on your lap yet, because we are not going until the bus is full with people. Wait until you see that the bus is close to being full."

"Did you already pay for the bus ticket?" the passenger asked.

"No, not yet," Estella answered.

"Good. Do what I have told you, because they will start collecting bus fees soon. Sometimes they do it on the way; sometimes they collect the fees before you enter the bus; and sometimes they collect the fees just after the bus starts moving. It all depends!"

"Thank you," Estella said.

"Don't thank me; thank my grandmother. She was the one who told me all these travelling tricks," the passenger answered, winking.

"Where are you from?" the passenger asked.

"Botswana. My name is Estella. You can call me also *Mama Felix*, if you want. My son's name is Felix," Estella said.

"They call me Mama Mulenga. I'm from *Lusaka*, the capital city of Zambia. My son Mulenga is in high school there. Botswana is a very good country. My brother is teaching there. Why are you coming to this country?" the passenger asked.

"Visiting my brother and sister in Zambezi Village. I might live with them," Estella explained.

"I see. I have never heard of that village. It must be small, yeh?" Mama Mulenga voiced, winking her eye and tilting her head towards Estella.

"Yes, my sister said it is quite small," Estella affirmed.

"Take your time, my sister. The bus won't leave soon until it gets full. The conductor said it would leave at 11:00 A.M. but I don't think so. So you can buy your son something to eat or drink on the road while we wait. It's going to be a long drive. If you go outside to get something, I can keep an eye on your luggage and make sure no one sits in your seat. I can look after Felix if you want as well," Mama Mulenga offered.

"How long it's going to take from here to Livingstone?" Estella asked.

"This is a new bus. It will take not more than two hours. In fact, an express bus from here to Livingstone should take an hour and fifteen minutes, but because this bus might stop in some towns along the way to pick up people who are going to Livingstone, we won't get there in that time," Mama Mulenga explained.

"I don't mind as long as we get there," Estella answered.

Around 11:45 A.M., the bus was full with passengers. The driver boarded the bus after everyone and started driving. Estella wondered where the bus conductor was as the bus pulled away from the station. Estella looked through her window and she saw the bus conductor running after them. The driver stopped to let the conductor onto the bus before he started driving again.

"J.J! What's going on?" The bus driver asked the bus conductor.

"Sorry boss, I went to buy some cigarettes. The guys we usually get them from were not there today," J.J. answered and handed the driver a lit cigarette.

"I was waiting for you. We should get this *lion* (referring to the bus) to Livingstone by 2:00 P.M.," the driver said, patting the worn steering wheel.

"I think we'll make it 2:00 P.M., Boss. It looks like all passengers that we have on the bus are going straight to Livingstone. So we may not stop in between and we can avoid the delays," J.J. discussed.

After twenty minutes on the journey, J.J. started to collect bus fees from the passengers. When he reached Felix and Estella, Felix was sitting on his mama's lap.

"Madam, fee?" J.J. asked.

Estella handed fifteen-pula money to the conductor.

"You are from Botswana? We do accept pula money but you have to pay five extra pula on this, as a service fee to exchange currencies. You are in Zambia; we use kwacha here," J.J. explained.

"I understand," Estella replied.

"How old is he?" J.J. asked.

"You mean my son, Felix?"

J.J. nodded.

"He is six years old," she answered.

"Okay, good. If he was 12 years or older, he would need to pay the fee even if he is sitting on your lap," J.J. said.

As the conductor moved on, Estella pointed out the bus window and showed Felix the landscape outside the bus. Felix saw swamps and shrubs. He saw also a variety of birds flying over the ground. Felix's eyes opened wide and he smiled.

"Wow, Mom! But I can't see elephants or other animals here," Felix said.

"Animals are kept and protected in game parks. If you are lucky, we might pass through a park and you might see some animals. Perhaps not elephants but others—maybe a hippo swimming in the Zambezi River," Estella said and winked at him.

A passenger who sat next to Estella and Felix got out of the bus when it stopped in a small town before Livingstone.

"You can let your son sit on my seat now, I don't see passengers from this station getting on this bus," he told Estella as he left the bus. Felix was happy. He settled onto the seat next to his mother. Soon after, the bus resumed its journey and left the small town.

****

The bus arrived in Livingstone before 2 P.M. At the bus station there, Estella and Felix climbed down out of the bus. Mama Mulenga also disembarked.

"Have a wonderful rest of your trip Mama Felix," said Mama Mulenga.

"Thank you," Estella said. She and Felix walked around the bus station. They sat and rested there for few minutes. Estella asked a stranger who sat next to them: "Where is the train station to Lusaka?"

"Over there! If you take this road; then that road; and then the next road, the station is just to your right, after the post office. It's within a very short distance. Ask if you get lost. People are very nice here," the man directed.

Estella and Felix were already feeling tired. Felix wanted to see elephants. He kept asking his mother to take him to a park where animals are kept. Estella kept telling him to wait until he and she reach Zambezi Village. The stranger heard Felix protesting to his mother about wanting to see an elephant.

"I can take you to a park, where you can see elephants," the stranger offered.

"It's okay. We don't have time. We have to leave for Lusaka today," Estella explained.

Felix's eyes welled up. He looked up and moaned entreatingly to his mother.

The stranger bent down and assured Felix: "It's okay, you can always visit Livingstone. There is also Victoria Falls here. *David Livingstone* died here. He is a white man from Scotland who brought Christianity to us. We are thankful for him. That's why we gave this place his name."

"Okay! Thank you for your advice," Estella said.

Estella told Felix they had to start walking to the train station. Felix was hesitant to stand up from the bench where he sat.

His mother said to him, "Felix, how do you know that there are no elephants where we are going?

"They are?" Felix asked.

"Lets go; you'll find out when we get there," she said.

They walked to the train station and fortunately

discovered that the train was leaving for Lusaka in one hour. Passenger trains followed scheduled times: A train left the station at its scheduled time of departure, whether it was full with passengers or not.

At the station, Estella went with Felix to a window that had a big white-mark sign on top of it: *"Tickets."* She bought two tickets from Livingstone to Lusaka: one for herself and another for Felix. The ticket seller accepted pula money.

In Livingstone, many businesses accepted foreign money from Zambia's southern neighbours, because of the many tourists from these countries who came to Livingstone to see Victoria Falls, Zambezi River, national parks and other things.

Estella's ticket cost her one hundred and twenty five pula. Felix was a child under twelve years old so thus his ticket only cost half as much. At the ticket shop, Estella also exchanged most of her pula money for kwacha.

"Where are you going?" the ticket seller asked Estella.

"We are going to Lusaka, but eventually ending up in Zambezi Village," Estella answered.

"Why not go straight to Copperbelt Province and catch a bus to Zambezi Village from there?"

"Well, we would like to stop in Lusaka first because we want to see the capital city. In Botswana, where we are coming from, we never lived in the capital. Who knows, maybe my son Felix can live there when he grows up. His father wanted him to be a *town boy*."

"Okay, it makes sense. Lusaka is a beautiful city," said the seller.

Estella heard a train horn. She asked the seller: "Is

that the train taking us to Lusaka?"

"Yes. That is the first signal: you should start getting on the train now. The second horn means the train is leaving," the seller advised.

Estella and Felix rushed through the station and onto the train. Both were excited. They pushed their luggage underneath their seat—a two-passenger bench with a window on the side. The train had washrooms and a food concession on board. In spite of this, people were selling food, drinks, and souvenirs like jewelry on the platform in front of the train. These sellers walked alongside the train and shouted the names of goods they sold at passengers through the windows of the train. A seller with buns shouted repeatedly while he walked: "nice, fresh and sweet buns for only *fifty ngwee* (half of one kwacha)!"

Estella bought six buns from one of the vendors and gave four buns to Felix. She also bought two soft drinks from another vendor who sold soft drinks and milk. She gave one soft drink to Felix and kept another soft drink for herself. Felix was happy. The second train horn sounded. The vendors moved away from the train carrying their goods. The train started to move.

Felix was tired, so he placed his head on his mother's lap and slept. After about two hours, just before the train reached another station, in the southern part of the country, the train conductor started to inspect passengers' train tickets. Passengers who did not have tickets were told to leave the train on a next station.

Estella was lonely. Felix was sleeping and none of the other passengers were talking to her. As she stared through the window, she thought about Pedro:

I wish I made this trip with you, when you were still alive.

Although this was during a cold season in Zambia, it was unseasonably sunny and windy outside the train. Tall grass on the flat land and branches from tall trees outside the train were waving along with the wind. Dry leaves were flying chaotically in the sky. Watching them gave her a momentary peace. *Maybe the wind and motion of the tree branches signify Pedro coming from the heavens telling me that all is going to be okay.*

Estella was worried about Felix's future and her little boy growing up without his father. But somehow she felt a little comforted by the landscape and nature along the railway tracks. It was as if the train trip was prearranged by higher powers. *If I can feel you now Pedro, maybe I can say goodbye.*

****

Before reaching Lusaka, the train stopped in other towns along the rail line. Some people disembarked in these towns and new passengers boarded the train. Felix woke up when the train was passing through towns in the southern area of the country. He pressed his nose against the window. When the train passed in this area, Felix was amazed to see large farms of sugarcanes.

"Mom look at the big grass over there!" he told Estella.

"No, that is not grass; those are sugarcanes. That's what sugar is made from," she explained.

Felix and Estella passed the bridge crossing the *Kafue River*. He grew excited again, this time to see the river and the escarpments along the rail line. His mother was quiet and tired, resting while she watched his happy face.

****

Finally, they reached Lusaka early the next morning. The train stopped and conductors allowed passengers to get off. The train was spending the night in Lusaka, before resuming its journey to the Copperbelt Province—its final destination.

Estella and Felix departed the train with their luggage. They felt a bit fatigued from sitting on the train for long hours. Nonetheless, they were happy to have arrived in Lusaka. The sunset was appearing; the sky was clear and red and the wind was blowing. People were walking, biking and boarding buses. It was a busy Tuesday morning.

The train station was located near an open-air market, where people sold all sorts of goods: clothes, food, cosmetics, electronics, household stuff and furniture.

It was time for Estella to shop around in Lusaka. Their final destination was *Zambezi Village,* a tiny rural community in the northwestern Zambia with limited variety of goods to buy. Estella had discovered on this journey that she loved shopping and travelling. In Botswana, she had never before had the freedom and time to shop as she had on this trip.

At the market, Estella bought new shoes for Felix and herself. She bought also cosmetics for herself, a shirt for her brother and a blouse for her sister.

Felix liked Lusaka. He asked his mother if he could go to school here.

His mother responded: "Maybe when you grow up Felix. You can come and study at a college here."

"But that is too long to wait, mother! Can't I start school here now?"

"We should first go and see your uncle and aunt in their village. Besides, it's good that you will have family to support you there. Here in Lusaka, there is no one I know to help us. That's why we have to go up to the village. It is a good thing to have familiar faces around you."

Felix trusted his mother. He knew that he was safe in his mother's good hands. He did not object to all of her advice.

Estella was proud of her six-year-old son. She wanted him to finish all of primary and secondary school, and go on to study at a college. Estella dreamed of Felix becoming a respected medical doctor. Estella believed that her son could have a highly-educated career now because she supported him. He lived in a safe country with no wars, unlike her home country of Angola, at that time. She considered Felix lucky to be growing up in a peaceful environment.

Around noon, Estella and Felix had rested enough in Lusaka. Estella decided to take a bus that was travelling straight from Lusaka to Zambezi Village. Estella did not want to take the train to Copperbelt Province because she wanted to arrive quickly to her siblings. She thought the train would take longer time to arrive in the Copperbelt Province than a bus.

On the route through the Copperbelt Province there were mining sites. She and Felix saw open pits and big trucks and bulldozers lifting and moving rocks around. Felix and Estella also saw mining refinery pipes producing thick white clouds.

Estella pointed with her right hand towards these

sights and exclaimed, "Felix, look! It looks like the mining area where we lived. That place you see over there—look! It is like the mining company where your father worked at before he passed away."

"I wish my daddy was here so that he could show me places like that. Maybe when I grow up I should go and work there!" Felix piped.

"Mom, how far is it from here to the place where we are going?" he asked.

"A couple of hours," Estella answered. "Felix, you have a long way to go before you decide what you want to be and where you want to work. Your interests might change. Don't you want to be doctor or a lawyer—someone people would respect?" Estella suggested.

"I guess. I don't even know what it looks like inside a mine. But it would be cool to drive those trucks on top of the hills there," Felix said.

After they were done talking about looking at the mines, Estella and Felix spent much of the time sleeping on the bus.

The bus stopped during the night in a small town in Copperbelt Province, before reaching its final destination, Zambezi Village.

The conductor told all the passengers: "It's late. We are not driving at night to our final destination. The clouds are dark and it might rain while we drive. It is simply not safe. We are going to spend a night here in the town, and we will resume our journey tomorrow morning. You can sleep on the bus or outside. There's a bus station, where you can also sleep. You can leave your luggage on the bus if you want. The bus will resume its journey at 5 A.M. tomorrow morning."

Passengers stepped out of the bus with their bags. Some went to the bus station to sleep on the benches there; some went to use washrooms at the station; others went to buy food and drinks; and still others remained on the bus and began to fall asleep. Estella and Felix bought some local food (cassava, groundnuts and mango juice), returned to eat on the bus. Then they covered themselves with quilts and slept.

CHAPTER 5

THE bus recommenced its journey to Zambezi Village the next morning, and Estella and Felix finally arrived at the *boma* (a central town near the village) around 9:00 A.M. The boma was a small town where people sold a variety of goods and services. Government-administrative tasks and other essential services were also carried out at the boma. Estella and Felix walked a dozen kilometers from the boma to go to their relatives' home in the village. About three hundred people, including Estella's siblings, lived in this tiny village. Most of the people in the village lived a simple lifestyle. There were also several other villages surrounding the boma. People from the surrounding villages came to the boma to trade goods and services.

There was no one from Estella's family at the boma to receive Estella and Felix. Estella's brother Ricardo and sister Gertrude did not know that Felix and Estella were arriving at that time. Estella and Felix got off the bus.

It was a sunny morning. The market at the boma was full of wooden tables and kiosks with vendors selling foods and other items. Some of the items for sale were placed on simple plastic mats on the ground.

"Mommy, I can smell fish. There are fish everywhere! Do they have an ocean nearby here?" Felix asked.

"No, Zambia is surrounded by land. It does not have an ocean. Perhaps people here get the fish from rivers or lakes. Angola, where your daddy and I came from, is by the Atlantic Ocean. Someday, when the war is over, we can visit Angola," said Estella.

"What about bananas? I see them everywhere and I can smell them too," Felix asked.

"Yes, people here grow bananas. Your uncle had told me that in one of his letters. That's why you see so many of them here for sale. People from other places come here to buy the bananas too," Estella answered.

"Are all these people I see buying bananas from somewhere else?" Felix asked.

"No, my son: not everyone here is buying bananas. See! There are many things people are selling on the market. Some are travelling to and from other places," said Estella.

Is this where we are going to live? Felix wondered silently.

As he walked with his mother, Felix stepped into a pothole and fell onto the ground. His clothes were covered in dust. Luckily, there was no concrete on the ground so Felix was not hurt. Estella helped him up and dusted him off.

"It's going to be okay, my son. We are going to

live with our family members, my sister and brother. They will love you and take care of you." Estella comforted Felix who was crying at this time.

At the market, they asked sellers there if they knew Gertrude and Ricardo. One of the sellers asked:

"What are their last names?"

Estella replied: "Sandona."

"Oh, I know a Sandona; we go to church together. He is a tall and slender man; maybe that's your brother," the seller said, gesturing with his finger at Estella.

"Can you take us to him?" Estella asked.

"Yes, sure," the seller replied and left his table, told his kiosk neighbour to look after his goods (dry fish) and started escorting Estella and Felix.

"My name is James Sakoza. I know that your brother is from Angola. I too came from Angola. People here call me Chief Sakoza," the seller introducing himself as he led them away from the market.

"We are just arriving here from Botswana. This is my son Felix. You can call me Mama Felix; I'm a sister to Gertrude and Ricardo," Estella introduced Felix and herself, briefly.

"Wow, what a long journey? You came all the way here? How is Botswana? Anyway, you must be tired by now. Let me get you to your family so that you rest first and then we can talk more later," Chief Sakoza said.

Estella, Felix and Chief Sakoza walked on a bush trail to Ricardo's house. The land was flat, and the trail was surrounded by wild grass and tall trees scattered across the area. Felix enjoyed seeing all the different scenery. As he walked in the trail, he saw things that he had not seen before. There were large trees with huge trunks—*Baobab* trees.

"Mom, do you hear the birds singing? I can hear their songs. Look, I see them there. They are flying. Look! Mom, see huts here and there. They are made of mud, not cement. There are not many houses here. Where are we going to live?" Felix asked his mother.

"Wait, you will see when we get to the house. I'll will show you," Estella directed.

Estella and Felix had seen houses made of mud before. However, Estella and Felix did not know they were going to live in a house made of mud.

****

According to Estella's memory, *Zambezi Village* was different than her former hometown in Botswana in several ways. Her former hometown in Botswana was a rapidly developing mining town. It had some houses with electricity and plumbing; and the government administration and lifestyles were based on urban standards. Unlike Zambezi Village, which was hundreds of kilometers away from large populations or modern cities.

There were no shopping malls, "modern" houses or technology, or major transportation systems. Colonial-style government or law enforcement did not exist in this village either. Population in the village was small (three hundred people scattered across the area) when compared to other densely populated places like Lusaka.

In this village, people governed themselves through traditional rulers called *chief heads*. Families solved family domestic disputes themselves. The chief heads solved community problems such as crime. If a person stole crops from a farmer, chief heads would call a meeting to discuss what type of punishment to which they would sentence the perpetrator. Punishments usually involved labouring for the farmer they stole from, and sometimes compensation in the form of harvest or livestock to their victim.

The life in the village was definitely a big change for Estella and Felix. This was a new beginning. Estella had not imagined that they would be living in a village or country lifestyle. But she saw that in order for them to survive, they needed to adapt to this livelihood and embrace it.

Like most people in this village, Estella's siblings earned their income from their small farm. They were small subsistence farmers: They sold few crops to earn an income. They were also involved in a barter system with other people in the village. For example, Estella's siblings exchanged their crops for other goods such as cooking oil, salt, sugar, candles and paraffin used in their lantern lamps.

As Estella, Felix and Chief Sakoza walked along the trail, birds were singing and the grass was waving gently, following wind directions across the flat land. Few insects were crawling over shrubs; butterflies were sunbathing on strands of wild grass and mobs of red ants were marching across the trail to unknown destinations in the bush fields. This was the trail Felix would use regularly to go to school and back.

As Felix ran around them exploring, Estella and Chief Sakoza met men and women walking with luggage on their heads and in wheelbarrows. Some were carrying farming tools such as hoes, and other people were on bicycles heading to the market at the boma. After two and half hours of walking, Estella, Felix and Chief Sakoza arrived at Ricardo's house. Ricardo was not there.

"Sandona, Sandona! You have guests here; your sister from Botswana is here," Chief Sakoza yelled.

Ricardo was chatting with Gertrude in her house, it was only a few meters away from his. Ricardo heard his name outside and said to Gertrude: 'I hear the voice of Chief Sakoza outside saying something; let us check."

Both Gertrude and Ricardo came outside the house and saw Estella and Felix and said, "Who are the visitors we have here?"

"Sandona! This is your family from Botswana. Can't you see how you all resemble one another?" Sakoza introduced, pointing his finger at everyone.

Gertrude ran and hugged Estella and Felix. "Oh, yes! Look at you, sister, you are looking well. Felix, you are such a grown-up little man. Welcome! Welcome! Come and sit here," Gertrude said.

She went in her house and brought stools and a mat made of dry bamboo trees. Felix, Chief Sakoza, and Ricardo sat on the stools. Estella and Gertrude sat on the mat. They all chatted about the journey from Botswana to Zambia. Chief Sakoza soon left, saying "See you in church," to Ricardo.

Gertrude prepared cooked cabbage and fish deep-fried with tomatoes and onions with *nshima* (made from corn and cassava flour). Felix, Gertrude, Estella and Ricardo sat and ate food.

In the evening before they went to bed, they went and sat in a patio that was independently built from the two main huts. The patio was located on the center of the yard between the two houses. It had an attic where the family stored dry food and cooking utensils. It is also where the family members gathered and held discussions, particularly during in the evenings and mornings.

Like Gertrude's hut, Ricardo's house had two rooms, a small bedroom and a living room used for many daily activities. Felix's uncle slept in his house's bedroom. Felix went and slept on a handmade wooden bed in Ricardo's living room.

As Felix walked through the house, he smelled fresh water from the well. The living room had a few things stacked against the walls—stored food and water and farming tools. Also, he could smell mud but did not know that it came from wet soil still clinging to the tools Ricardo had used that day. He looked up and all he could see was darkness in the roof. The roof was made of dry tree sticks and wild grass.

At night, before Felix was asleep, he heard *cicada* insects making prolonged songs. In the morning, Felix was awakened by roosters. These were all new experiences for Felix. But he was not bothered by these noises. He appreciated nature. He felt for the first time that he was part of it and lived in it.

Ricardo was not married and did not have children. He had a girlfriend named Josephine who lived in the village. He could not live with her because he was not married to her and her parents did not allow Ricardo to live with Josephine. Ricardo could not afford the bride price that Josephine's parents asked from him—two cows, four goats and another house for Josephine's parents.

Gertrude and Estella went and slept in Gertrude's house. Gertrude was a single mother just like her sister. She had a twelve-year-old daughter named Lucy, Felix's cousin. Lucy was not there when Estella and Felix arrived. She was in Solwezi. Lucy was in grade six, attending a boarding school in Solwezi, about four hours drive from Zambezi Village.

CHAPTER 6

IN 1977, the same year Estella and her six-year-old Felix arrived in the village, Estella had asked Ricardo to enroll Felix in a primary school in the area. So the following morning, Ricardo took Felix to a local school near the boma, about two-hour-walking distance from the village. Felix and Ricardo chatted as they walked.

"Today, we are going to register you in school. First, we need to go to the boma to get a national registration number for you," Ricardo said.

"Uncle, what's boma?" Felix asked.

"The boma is the central town, where many official things are done, things such as getting your national registration number. English people used the boma as their main office for governing the people around this area. Many places have their own boma. For example, Lusaka, the place you passed through as you came here, also has a boma," Ricardo explained.

"Uncle, I would like to work at the boma; can I also work here when I grow up," Felix said.

He added: "Uncle, where do you work?"

Ricardo fell silent after listening to Felix's questions. He looked down while he was walking. He felt somewhat ashamed that he had never finished secondary schooling. He wondered whether he was a good role model for Felix or not. He realized that Felix had a great chance to finish schooling. Ricardo did not want that potential to be wasted.

Ricardo explained: "Here, many people would call me a *"grade-seven failure;"* because, I did not finish secondary school. I failed school in grade seven. That's why I'm just a subsistence farmer. Here, you go to a primary school where you attend grade one to seven; then, you have to write grade-seven national school examinations in order to proceed to grade eight in secondary school. I attended primary school from grade one to seven, but I failed grade-seven national school examinations. So, I did not go to grade eight. Don't be like me. Go to school! Finish school! Your mom is right: You will do many things with school. You will get a good job. You will be a manager of a big company, or a manager at a mine in the Copperbelt Province. You will make good money. Finish grade one and all the way to twelve! I know that you are clever; you will finish and do well in school."

Felix appeared thoughtful also. He listened, as well. Ricardo walked with Felix to the boma, which was about twelve kilometers from their hut. At the boma, Felix obtained a national registration number, a prerequisite for first grade registration. Ricardo and Felix walked another distance of two kilometers to the primary school, where Felix was finally registered.

The school registration was done in the school

headmaster's office. When Felix and Ricardo arrived, there was a line of adults with children who were also registering for school. Ricardo and Felix waited for an hour. Then the headmaster opened his office door, and an adult and child left the office.

"Who's next?" the headmaster asked.

"Me," Ricardo answered.

"Come on in then. Sit down please," the headmaster offered while he sat in his chair.

There was a brown metal desk between his chair and two guest chairs, where Ricardo and Felix sat. There was a national flag on the headmaster's desk, and on the office wall there was a portrait of the state president of that time.

"How old is he?" the headmaster asked, pointing his pen at Felix.

"I'm six years old." Felix answered.

"Is he six?" the headmaster asked.

"Yes, he is six," Ricardo replied.

"Okay, give me the national registration number," the headmaster instructed.

Ricardo gave the headmaster the number.

After, the headmaster said: "I am going to put you in Mrs. Kano's class in room 12. Okay? Come tomorrow at seven o'clock with five books (one for each subject you will be taking) and two pencils—all that in a student briefcase. Please come to school wearing a complete proper school uniform. That's it."

On their way home, Ricardo and Felix stopped at the boma to buy Felix's school uniform. Estella had given Ricardo some money to spend on Felix's school items. Ricardo bought Felix's school-uniform clothes: blue shorts, white shirt, blue sweater, black shoes and blue socks. Ricardo bought the shoes and socks from a shoe kiosk, and the shirt, sweater and shorts from the local tailor.

Felix was excited to see the school uniform. He wanted to wear the clothes immediately. Ricardo also bought some dried tiger fish. They returned home and gave the fish to Felix's aunt. Gertrude cooked the fish that night for their supper meal. Felix tasted the fish for the first time in his life. He told his uncle that the fish was delicious and tasty. Felix began loving life in the village.

****

Felix's uncle showed Felix where his school was located. Like most boys in the village, it was time for Felix to start being independent. On his first school day, Felix put on his school-uniform clothes and began his school life. He walked to and from school by himself. The school had limited school materials, such as books, desks, chalk, pens and pencils. There were not many teachers at the school. One teacher had forty to sixty students in one class building. Some students sat on the floor in class. Due to limited school materials in the classes, teachers took students outside for lessons. Students used the outside environment to learn how to write, draw and count. Felix learned how to write by writing on the ground using fallen tree branches. He also learned addition and subtraction through counting stones and sticks.

On Felix's first day at school, Felix and other students were in class with their teacher, Mrs. Beatrice Kano. The school bell rang and Mrs. Kano instructed the students to join the parade outside the classroom. She and the other teachers as well as the school-deputy headmistress and headmaster also came to the parade.

Every morning, students formed a school parade before they began their classes. The parade consisted of straight queues of students; each school grade formed its own queue, from grade one to seven. Schoolteachers, the headmistress and headmaster, and other school officials stood in front of the parade on a podium. The podium's center had a long metal pole with the national flag.

"*Stand up straight!*" the school-deputy headmistress commanded. At the parade, teachers inspected their students to make sure they had groomed themselves and had dressed in proper school uniforms. Students who had not combed their hair or cut their nails or had not dressed appropriately were punished by working in the school garden or classroom cleaning. In rare circumstances, some students were expelled from the school—if they did something that was extremely unacceptable like fighting in the classroom. Felix did not want to do anything considered inappropriate at the school. He did not want to be expelled from the school, and neither to disappoint his mother and uncle.

After the inspection, the students and teachers sang the national anthem and the headmaster spoke to the students about the students code of conduct.

"You must arrive early to school and start classes on time. You are forbidden from using any local slang. You are only allowed to speak English on the school grounds. Noisiness, lateness and bad manners will not be tolerated in this school," the headmaster commanded.

The students responded: *"Yes sir!"*

On that afternoon, the headmaster also informed the students, the president of the country would be visiting the school, as part of his mission to empower children's national identity.

The headmaster informed: "It is a great pleasure to announce to you that you will have a chance to meet with the president of our nation today. The visit will take place this afternoon around twelve o'clock. Make sure you behave well. The president may ask one of you or all of you about our great country and our national symbols. You must know the capital city of this country and most importantly the meaning of our coat of arms and flag. Remember this. Your teachers can prepare you further—for the presidential visit."

After the address, the students were dismissed from the parade. They walked quietly in queues to their respective classes. Classes were held for five hours, from 7:00 A.M. to 12:00 P.M.

Felix looked around in the class of both girls and boys. He was excited to be in school but felt somewhat forlorn. His body looked healthy and he had a medium-size height. He was a fairly chubby boy with oily skin and black thick hair. He had a regular-shaped face. In the class, he hoped that a student would come and befriend him, but no student approached him to talk or play with him that day.

Felix did not sit on a desk. He and a few other students sat on the stones in class. Felix felt homesick. He was sucking his right thumb and he was looking down as he sat on the stone. Mrs. Kano noticed that Felix was lonely.

"Felix, are you okay?" Mrs. Kano asked.

"Yes," Felix said.

"I understand it's your first day of school. Are you

from around here?" Mrs. Kano asked again.

"I live here now; my mom and I came from Botswana. I like this place. It's very nice," Felix replied.

"Oh, Botswana. It is a beautiful country. What brought you to this country?" she asked.

"My mother has family living here. We wanted to live close with the family. That's why we came," Felix repeated.

"You will be okay. Ask me if you need anything; I can help," Mrs. Kano said.

Felix's eyes widened. He felt relaxed.

On his first school day, Felix was supposed to go home at 12:00 P.M. when his class was dismissed, but he did not. Felix waited for the president to visit the school. Around 1:00 P.M., Felix saw a presidential motorcade carrying the president, who was waving a white handkerchief through the window of his car. Felix rushed to the school parade.

The president went to the podium and addressed the students on the parade. He made an empowering speech to students regarding unity, good citizenship and the goodness of the country.

The president then left the school. He went to visit another school in the nearby area.

Felix was impressed by the president's presentation. Felix felt encouraged by the speech, also. Felix thought to himself, *unity is important*. He began to develop a strong sense of belonging to the country. He felt supported by the president. Felix began to realize that he was not alone but among others in the country. And then Felix felt included in the school.

The love Felix received from his mother was not

by words or hugs or kisses. Felix knew that his mother loved him. He did not need to measure his mother's love to him. Felix's intuition and memories of her presence throughout his life showed him that his mother loved him.

Felix felt his mother loved him; she protected and cared for him when his father died. She did not abandon him. That was essential to Felix. Because of this, he did not want to ask more things from his mother. He felt that she did more than enough, taking care of him all on her own. He contemplated that asking his mother for extra things he wanted in his life would question the significance of his mother's love towards him and *asking* would put pressure on his mother. He understood that when his father Pedro died, all the burden fell upon Estella.

Throughout primary school, Felix did not have many friends to play with. Instead, he played mostly at his home with his uncle's goats and chickens. Behind the house, Ricardo had a chicken coop that had roosters, and both young and old chickens. He had also a small "V" shaped goats' shed with twelve goats in it. Both the coop and shed were made of dry tree branches from bamboo plants, and the roofs were covered with bundles of wild grass.

The coop was built three meters horizontally away from the ground. The coop had a small ladder (also made of bamboo sticks), which the chickens used to climb into the coop. Ricardo and Felix also used the ladder to climb to the coop when they wanted to clean or fix it. Ricardo wanted his hens to lay their eggs in the living room, so that he could protect them. So he made nests for the hens inside his house. The nests were made of basins. The basin bottoms

An African Orphan

were covered with soft clothing and dry wild grass. The hens used these nests to lay their eggs and slept there afterwards, as long as Ricardo would let them.

The chicken pecked mostly in the yard at home. Sometimes they went into the bush near the house to eat wild food. The yard had a couple of trees spread around it. There was also an anthill located about ten meters away from the front of Ricardo's house. Felix did not like the chicken to go into the bush, because on many occasions he witnessed tiny chicks killed by eagles and bitten by ants. The bush was located a few meters away from the yard. Felix enjoyed chasing chicken within the yard. Felix liked to play tag with hens and chicks. He chased chicks with hens; he grabbed one or two chicks; and he ran with them around the yard. The hens were furious from losing their chicks. The hens chased him until he released the chicks back to them. Felix felt exuberated every time he played this wild chase.

Felix discovered chicken were also clever creatures; they had feelings; they did not want pain. It seemed to Felix that whenever he ate chicken eggs, the hens that laid those eggs became angry. He also realized that the hens did not like him to be near their nests. The hens became aggressive and jumped at him whenever he was near the nests. The hens also ran to hide every time they saw an eagle. Sometimes the hens fought with eagles.

In the evening (without directions from Felix), the chicken climbed up the ladder to their coop and went to sleep. That amazed Felix. The goats also went to sleep by themselves, but sometimes they needed a reminder from Felix.

He would scold them: "Go to sleep! Tomorrow

comes early!"

These were new and exciting experiences for Felix. Perhaps the most important lesson Felix learned was that animals were each different from the other; and they all wanted to be treated with dignity, respect and fairness.

Because Felix no longer had a father, Ricardo (Felix's uncle) felt responsible to be a male role model for Felix. Consequently, Ricardo wanted to instill manly values and skills in Felix. Ricardo reasoned that, because Felix was a boy, Felix was bound to have aptitudes for farming, hunting, fishing and animal husbandry. So Ricardo started to take Felix to his fields and out to fish in a local river and swamps.

****

A few years passed, Felix was ten years old. He continued to enjoy the village lifestyle, its simplicity and rich meaning.

One day, during the rainy season of 1981, Ricardo took the ten-year-old Felix to his farm. The farm was about five kilometers from Ricardo's house. While Ricardo and Felix walked to the farm, Ricardo showed him different types of birds that were playing in the bush. Ricardo told Felix that birds sang songs that had a meaning in the village. For example, one particular bird sang a song that said: *"There are teachers in this village."*

Ricardo and Felix arrived back at the farm. Ricardo showed Felix how to weed corn.

"Hold this hoe, upright, and weed like this. Do these three lines of corn. I will be over there behind that anthill, where I will be digging cassava roots out from the ground for supper," Ricardo instructed.

Felix was happy that he had been given some of the responsibilities that his uncle shouldered. But after half an hour of weeding, Felix felt tired. He looked around in the farm; he did not see his uncle. Felix walked behind the anthill; he did not see his uncle there. At this time, Felix was scratching his right leg. He had stepped on red ants. His leg started to burn more.

Panicking, Felix screamed: "Uncle, uncle! Where are you?"

"I'm here," Ricardo answered.

"Where?" Felix said.

"Here, over here—under the tree," Ricardo said.

Felix rushed to where the voice was coming from. While he was walking, he stepped on a group of small non-venomous snakes and one bit his right knee. Felix was feeling faint and dramatic.

Why did we come here? he thought. Felix started to cry. His uncle came and saw Felix crying.

"What happened?" Ricardo asked.

"Snakes and ants bit me here," Felix showed his leg.

"Stay still; sit down. Show your leg to me," Ricardo said.

Ricardo cut a few long green grasses and used the grass to tie Felix's right calf and shin. Ricardo also used a sharp stone from the ground and made a small cut on Felix's right knee and allowed some blood to flow out of the cut. Ricardo chewed bitter leaves he took from the bush, spat the chewed leaves on the cut and rubbed them against the skin.

"You are lucky, Felix. It wasn't a *Black Mamba* snake that bit you. The ant bites on your skin will go away after a while," Ricardo said.

But Felix was in pain. His temperature increased.

"Can you walk?" Ricardo asked.

"I don't know," Felix whimpered.

Ricardo lifted Felix. Felix sat on Ricardo's shoulders. Ricardo walked with Felix to their home. When they reached home, Estella saw Felix on Ricardo's shoulders and dry blood on Felix's leg.

"What happened?" Estella asked.

"He was bitten by the snakes and ants," Ricardo answered.

"Is he gonna be alright?" she cried anxiously.

"He will be fine. They weren't poisonous snakes. I tied his legs as well. He is okay," Ricardo explained.

It was evening and getting dark. Ricardo placed Felix on a bamboo mat in the patio and put the cassava roots he had dug up from the farm into a big cooking pot. He made a fire in the patio's fire pit and placed the pot on top. Estella had prepared nshima for Felix and Ricardo, before they came home.

"Are you going to eat the nshima I prepared for you?" Estella asked.

"Yes," Ricardo answered. Gertrude was not home. She went to visit her church friend who lived within the village.

Ricardo, Felix and Estella sat in the patio and Ricardo told stories about developments that were happening in the village. Ricardo was a member of a committee that was devoted to preserving ancient trees. He and Chief Sakoza attended the meetings of this project on Sundays, after church service.

Felix's eyes began to droop.

"Felix, are you sleepy?" Ricardo asked.

"I'm not. I'm just tired," Felix insisted.

"You should eat cassava before you sleep," Ricardo said.

"First let's eat the nshima your mom prepared. But leave some for your aunt, Gertrude. The cassava I'm cooking here is very good. It is the brown one, *father of fathers' cassava;* it is the Angolan breed. Lots of starch," Ricardo stated.

Estella asked, "Felix, can I cook some soup for you? Anyway, I will prepare some goat-bone soup, you would enjoy, okay?"

"Thank you mom. Soup would be lovely," Felix answered tenderly.

She cooked the soup and gave it to Felix and told him: "You will be well my son. You are a strong young man. Everything will be ok." Then she patted him on his head and gently ruffled his hair. And she sat close to him in the patio.

Cassava was still being cooked on the fire pit. Felix felt comfortable drinking the soup with his family in the warm patio.

Ricardo told folk stories to Felix while he was resting in the patio.

After Ricardo finished telling a third story to Felix, about "keeping promises," Ricardo asked Felix: "What have you learned from this story?"

Felix had been dozing while listening. But he replied, "Uncle, this is a good story. Can you tell me again tomorrow evening?"

"Yes," Ricardo said.

"The moral lesson of the story is that a man does not make promises that he cannot keep," Ricardo added. But Felix was already sound asleep. That night Felix did not eat cassava his uncle cooked. Ricardo saved some of the cassava for Felix to eat on the following day. After that night Felix was feeling better.

The next day after school, Ricardo gave Felix one young goat to look after. Felix was responsible for the welfare of that kid. Before he took on that responsibility, Felix was instructed by his uncle to name the kid. Felix had to name the goat a name that had a meaning to Felix, but more importantly the name had to fit the kid's character and appearance.

Felix named the goat *Generous*. Felix thought the goat was kind and gentle. Also, he used the name 'Generous' because his mother had always taught him about the importance of generosity to others.

Every time Felix saw the goat unhappy, he attended to the goat: he massaged Generous and took him on a leash to graze in the bush. Felix had to make sure also that the goat did not fall into the three ground holes that were in the backyard: a latrine, garbage trench, and an unfinished water well.

Felix connected well with Generous. They both listened to each other. Generous followed Felix's instructions, especially when he was told to go to sleep or eat food. Felix knew Generous's father and mother. Felix was friendly to all of them.

****

The following year, Felix was going to be a grade-six schoolboy. On that New Year's Day, Ricardo told Felix that Generous's father had to be killed for food. Felix's feelings were torn between the excitement of eating goat meat and the grief for Generous's father. It was another lesson Ricardo had to teach Felix. Ricardo wanted to show Felix how to kill a goat and prepare it for food. Although Felix did not like to kill an animal, he had to do it to please his uncle.

Like many young people in the village, Felix liked outdoor activities. He enjoyed climbing trees, especially mango and avocado trees. He climbed to the very tops to sit and eat the fruits there. Sometimes, he climbed onto the trees so that he could see the entire village from up high.

On occasions, Felix also climbed on the anthill, which was very close to his house. The anthill was not too high for him to climb. It was only few meters above the ground and its circumference base was also a couple meters around. However, most of the times, Felix found the anthill too steep to climb. He would slip down one foot after another as he climbed. For him, that was fun. He felt a sense of accomplishment every time he reached to the top of the hill. He enjoyed exercising his muscles by clinging and fighting his way to the top. From there, he was able to see the roofs of his hut, chicken coop and goat shed. Seeing those things from the top of the hill gave Felix a sense of control and possibility.

Tobias Mwandala

CHAPTER 7

THE dry season of 1982, the eleven-year-old Felix went to swim in a river that was a few kilometers away from his home. At the river he found four other boys around his age swimming naked in the water. Felix removed his clothes so that he could also swim. The other boys noticed that Felix was not circumcised. They started laughing at him.

"Look, look! He is not circumcised.

Felix rushed out of the river. He took his clothes and ran back to his home. Before he arrived home, he stopped running to step off the bush trail. He got redressed before finishing the journey to his home.

When Felix arrived at the house, his uncle was not there. His mother was at home. Felix could not talk to his mother about the experience he had at the river that day. At this time, he was aware that the subjects of his genitals or sex were only to be discussed with men—and not with women. So he did not talk to his mother about his experience with the boys at the river.

Felix was feeling ashamed. He felt that he was an outcast among the boys in his community. He also felt isolated. He wished his father was still alive.

If my father were here, the boys at the river would have not ridiculed me, he thought. *Why did my father have to die before I grew up?*

Estella approached Felix after she saw that he was sad.

"What's the matter?" she asked.

"I wish my father were here," he answered.

"Why?" Estella asked.

"I have noticed that other boys in the village have... things I don't have," Felix disclosed.

"They say to be in front does not always mean you are at your final destination. And sometimes where God gives, there is no smoke to show what he has done. God does not disappoint those who ask him," she advised.

Felix listened. He was not completely satisfied with his mother's advice, however. He wanted to share the experience he had at the river with his uncle.

Felix's uncle Ricardo had gone to attend a village meeting. On the way back home, he collected wood from the bush to bring home to their fire. Along the bush path, he met a friend he attended church with, Mr. Zuze.

Mr. Zuze asked: "I heard that your nephew is living with you. Is that right?"

"Yes, that's right," said Ricardo.

"My son needs to go the *initiation ceremony*." This was a circumcision ritual for young boys.

"He is at that age now. If Felix has not already gone through the ceremony, then they can do it together. Another friend of mine has two boys who also need to go through the ceremony," Mr. Zuze discussed.

"This is a good idea. I will let Felix's mother know about this opportunity. We are behind, in fact. The boy is growing. If we don't do this quickly, the whole village, my colleagues and family, will shame us. We, the men, should lead for these boys on this important issue," Ricardo expressed.

"This would never happen in Angola. For us, I remember that we went to the ceremony at a very young age. And, in those days, we went into the bush (the initiation ceremony) for two months, without seeing our parents," Ricardo said.

"Six years of age, that is when I went to the ceremony," said Mr. Zuze.

"The kids are lucky today. There are doctors who perform circumcision now. In fact, we have one doctor in our village that does this. He can do our boys at a cheaper rate, I think. My wife talks to him at the church and he seems to be friendly. I will arrange this with him; okay? You can arrange elders to be with our boys during the time in the bush. We will share the cost after. We need to send our boys to the bush during this next school holiday for sure. We are already late," Mr. Zuze repeated.

"Yes; my nephew Felix is eleven years old now. He is behind," Ricardo said. "We will talk further about setting up the ceremony for the boys."

Ricardo arrived at his house in the evening time. Felix was not at the house. Estella was at home knitting a blanket. Ricardo asked Estella about where Felix was. Estella told Ricardo that Felix had gone for a walk in the bush.

"Is everything okay?" Ricardo asked.

"Felix seemed very sad today. He was upset with me. He broke his father's radio when you were not here. I was not happy about that. He stopped listening to me, maybe because I'm his mother. He told me that he wants to talk to his father and not me," Estella shouted angrily.

After Ricardo listened to Estella, he went to look for Felix in the bush. He found Felix walking in the bush trail. Felix was crying about his father. He told Ricardo that he did not want to be in the village any longer.

"Come here. What's the matter?" Ricardo asked.

"I feel like I don't belong here. I feel alone in this village. No one loves me. I'm an outcast. All boys I've met are circumcised, except me," Felix mumbled into his uncle's chest as Ricardo hugged him.

"I understand how you feel. You miss your dad," Ricardo nodded. "I need to talk to you about something important to you as a man."

"Ok, I am listening," said Felix.

"I want you to go to the male bush for circumcision. It is time. You are now a grown up. You will spend one month and Josh, an elder friend of mine will be your guidance counselor there during that time. He will teach you, and you can go to him whenever you need anything. While you are in the bush, you won't be allowed to visit us. And, you will not be allowed to go to the village whatsoever.

"Also, you will be unable to eat meat, change clothes or see or talk to females during that time. After one month you will have healed, and you can come back to the village as a man. You will be no longer a child. You will need to show that you are different from people who have not been to the bush and people who are not from our tribe. Going to the bush will help you: you will be able to withstand challenges in life and you will be a stronger man. So? What do you think?" Ricardo asked.

"I was waiting to tell you that I want to go to the ceremony. All my age mates in this village have already been to the ceremony," Felix stated.

****

The following month during school holidays, Felix took part in the initiation ceremony. This was the most important ritual Felix ever undertook.

Every year there were one or more groups of boys who went to the bush and spent one month or more there. Almost all the boys in this village had gone through that process. To not go to the ceremony brought shame on the males in that village.

In that village, only initiation through this process was considered authentic. The 'bush' was merely a camp house for boys who went for the ceremony. This bush was located within the village. However, people in the village were not supposed to know where the bush was located, except initiated male family members of the boys in the bush. No other person was allowed to go to the bush or near it. It was a sacred place. Organizers of the ceremony considered it a dishonor to the spirits of the ritual when a non-initiated individual visited the bush or went near it. In the village, there were three other candidates of the ceremony who went with Felix to the bush at that time.

On the day Felix entered the bush, there were celebrations in the village. The celebrations involved previous graduates of the initiation ceremony and families of the new initiates of the ceremony. Outside the bush, there were people called "*masked.*" The *masked* dressed in traditional costumes: veiled faces with wooden masks and bodies covered with coloured-contoured cotton. The shape and size of the masks resembled wild-animal faces such as of those of a hyena, lion or elephant.

It was believed by the local people that dead spirits came to visit the living in form of animals. The majority of the people in the village did not know individuals that wore the *masked* masks. The people did not pay attention or care to know who was wearing the masks. Instead, the people focused on understanding the representation and meaning of the *masked*. This focus seemed essential to the people in that culture.

The *masked* danced around; some of them chased young people and others played folk guessing games with the people. Felix's community believed that the *masked* personages represented the spirits of the dead. For that reason, many young people (including Felix) were afraid of the *masked*.

Felix understood that these masked characters were sacred and they came to the world to bring back knowledge of the ancestors and culture to the present society, as well as to empower children and oppressed people. The *masked* had the power to send boys who were not initiated to the bush, without consent from boys' parents. For this reason, boys who surrounded these personages made sure they were initiated and had some knowledge about the questions of the guessing game. Masked characters also played with the people. For example, if a *masked* asked a question to a boy and the boy was unable to answer, then the *masked* would sent the boy to the initiation ceremony for further learning about the culture, whether the boy was initiated or not. Just before Felix went to the bush, he avoided being surrounded by the *masked*. He respected this ritual.

In some way, the masked characters gave Felix a sense of belonging. He understood that he came from a distinctive culture that had deeper values than ordinary ones. During the initiation, Felix also came to believe that he was not alone: His culture was much bigger than himself. He was living in a community of people with a history and values that existed before he was born. He became aware that he was only a unit among many other units of that community. Its entirety was more important than him, he reckoned. As a result, his identity became stronger. His ideas became less egotistical. He began to think about the world at large. He thought about others more than himself.

Felix spent one month in the bush. In the bush, he learned further about hunting and male manners, such as fatherhood—how to be a good husband, how to deal with a conflict and to treat people with respect and dignity.

During the initiation ceremony, Josh (Felix's bush-guidance counsellor) also told Felix that he was forbidden to enter his mother's bedroom, as a sign of respect to his mother. He was prohibited as well from engaging in what were called 'female' roles, such as cooking and sweeping, when females were present. "Doing so would constitute weakness upon an initiated man," Josh indicated. "Only perform womanly duties when females are not present."

Each boy in Felix's group had his own guidance counsellor. A guidance counsellor was responsible for the welfare of his student. The counsellor made sure food and lessons were provided to the student. Sometimes, before sleep, the counsellors and their students met in one group to share stories, riddles and proverbs, and many days passed.

Felix had a bad dream one night. In the morning he shared details about his dream with Josh.

"Last night, I dreamed about a huge black snake chasing me. I felt scared," Felix said.

Josh advised him, "In order for you to avoid bad dreams like that, place a small piece of charcoal near your head while you sleep. That will scare bad spirits away at night and you won't have bad dreams."

Felix did what Josh told him. He placed a piece of charcoal near his head before he fell asleep. Felix did not have bad dreams that night, and he continued to use Josh's advice every night after that.

In the bush, Felix had to cook for himself. One day, Josh saw Felix using a knife to stir relish he was cooking in a pot.

"You should never use a knife to stir food when cooking," Josh scolded him.

"Why?" Felix asked, widening his eyes.

"Well, stirring food with a knife can cause pain to your heart, after eating the food," Josh explained.

"Also, don't taste food while you are cooking it on fire because that will bring bad luck on you."

After that, Felix did not stir food with a knife any more. He started using a wooden spoon instead, and he never tasted food while it was cooking on fire.

At the end of the month, Felix was feeling that he was a grown man. Before dawn on the day of initiation graduation, Felix and the other graduates burnt the camp and all the old clothes they wore during the initiation month. The boys walked away from the bush. As they walked out from the bush, they did not look back. Looking back meant bad luck and a return to their old life, which was forbidden.

In order to wash away their childhood and bad luck, Felix and other graduates went to a nearby river and immersed themselves in the water without looking back. After, they dressed in new clothes.

Felix and the boys had to look forward. Felix was feeling rejuvenated. His life was revived. Felix was very happy to have gone through the initiation ritual. The boys' families and friends gathered at Ricardo's house. They prepared food and wine and invited other people in the village to receive the boys from the graduation. The people celebrated the boys' graduation for the initiation ceremony. It was now that Felix finally began to form new friendships from the bush and later in the village.

****

When Felix was twelve years old, he wrote grade seven national school examinations. The following year, 1984, he went to check the results of the examinations. It was a normal pattern for students to wait for their exam results months after they write their exams. The school posted the results on the doors of the classrooms. Felix went and saw his name on the door of his classroom. The name was among those who passed the examinations. Felix went to his headmaster's office to get full grade seven examination results. The headmaster presented his full examination results to Felix.

"I'm proud of a young man like you, Felix. You have been chosen to go to Zambezi Secondary School, where you will be studying grade eight and I know you will finish grade twelve as well. Please keep up with the good work. We need people like you in this country—who will be doctors, teachers, engineers and so on." the headmaster said.

"Thank you sir. I will work hard," Felix responded.

As soon as Felix left the office, he looked very closely at the examination results on the paper in his hand. Felix saw that he had passed his examinations with good grades. Felix had achieved excellent grades and merits in geography, civics, mathematics and science subjects, and satisfactory grades in home economics, English, and agriculture subjects. On the paper there was also the name of the secondary school he was assigned to, where he was to complete grades 8-12.

CHAPTER 8

FELIX'S mother also encouraged Felix to be a responsible person. One day, when Felix was thirteen years old, she told him that he was a man, and as a result, he needed to think for himself and assume "manhood" responsibilities. He needed to take care of himself and others. This idea was not foreign to Felix. He had already received similar instructions from his uncle and Josh.

Estella was a single mother who had not finished post-secondary school. This was one of the reasons she expected Felix to study hard in school. Felix's mother was ambitious. She was a strong and independent woman. Although she would have liked to have a traditional two-parent family for Felix, she enjoyed making decisions alone, especially regarding Felix's wellbeing and values.

Throughout her life, she advised Felix to marry his education. From her perspective, education was a priority before everything else. Felix remembered this message, especially when he faced hard choices in his life. He recalled his mother telling him, "Son, finish school before you get married."

Felix was guided by this message whenever he felt confused about which direction to take. But Felix was frustrated when his instinctual decisions conflicted with his mother's advice. He felt that he was missing a big part of being a young boy. He wanted to play and have fun. At these times, he did not follow his mother's voices. Instead he followed his friends: he intermingled with friends who did not believe in schooling.

Estella wanted Felix to be somebody, she used to say. For her, *somebody* meant a person with a post-secondary education and a career with a substantial steady income. She placed a great deal of importance on taking school seriously, getting good grades and travelling to different places. She saw that other adults around her were able to do these things with their education, and she wanted the same good life for her son.

One day, Felix told his mother that school was boring because he did not have fancy toys, uniforms, pencils and books, which a few other students had at his school. Felix did not want to go to school. He was grumpy and refused to bath, brush his teeth or put on his uniform. At that time, Felix felt schooling was not enjoyable for him. Sometimes, Felix felt "left out," especially when he saw other students who came with their fathers to parent-teacher meetings. And from time to time, Felix wished his father were alive.

On this day, Estella told a story to her son:

"I had a neighbour in Botswana who did not have two parents. A single foster mother raised him. He did not have anything to call his own. He went to school barefoot and wore a second-hand uniform. Sometimes he didn't eat breakfast or lunch or supper. Then he would be hungry when he got to school and still hungry when he went to bed that night. But he studied hard. He completed high school with flying colours. He went to university, and finished his education and became a prominent government official in Botswana. My son, you can do it too. You don't have to have all material goods and two parents in life in order to succeed."

Felix stopped crying. He sat down and looked at his mother while she talked. He listened intently to the story.

After, Felix asked his mother: "Where is the neighbour now?"

"He is still working as a minister in Gaborone," Estella answered.

Felix felt motivated by Estella's story. He bathed and dressed up in his uniform and went to the school that morning.

Estella had used up all the money she was given in Botswana. She was worried all of the time now. She wondered whether she was able to afford school tuition for Felix in a secondary school and college.

For that reason, Estella started a small business of selling second-hand clothing in the village. She also wanted to start a business because she enjoyed travelling and being busy. She wanted to spend time away from home when Felix was at school.

"I want to start a business to buy and sell second-hand clothing. I have an acquaintance from this village that buys second-hand clothes from the border between Zaire and Zambia, and sells them in Solwezi town.

"Can we go together?" Felix asked.

"This is for adults only, but when you grow up, I can take you once in a while," Estella stated.

"Please, please take me now," Felix pleaded.

Estella borrowed money from a man called Dr. Kamashi, whom she met at her church, and made her first trip to the border. The border was not too far from the village. She was not successful in her business, though. She used all the money from her business to pay Felix's grade-eight tuition fees.

****

In 1985, when Felix was fourteen years old, Estella fell into depression and hopelessness. Although her family surrounded Estella, she felt lonely. She felt that she did not belong there. In addition, she felt no sense of being. She lost her identity after Pedro's devastating death. Estella did not discuss these feelings with her family. She thought her family would not understand her.

Estella's health started to deteriorate. Estella stopped eating well. Her sleep pattern became unhealthy. And even when she fell asleep, it was not a *good* sleep. Her body became frail. Her mind became weak. She started to experience hallucinations. She stopped washing her clothes. She began to dress dirty clothes and stopped keeping up with good hygiene. Soon Felix began to notice these changes in his mother.

Felix was in an undecided state: whether to be at home with his mother or continue going to school. He knew that his mother wanted him to be in school no matter what. However, he did not know if that included the present situation, with Estella sinking further into depression. This was the biggest and most challenging moral decision he had faced in his young life. *Should I continue going to school despite my mother's illness; or should I stay home to care for her?*

Gertrude suspected that some witches in the village had cursed Estella. So she decided to go and consult with a village witch doctor whose name was Kokoya.

"What can I do for you?" Kokoya asked.

"My sister is very sick; I need to know what happened to her. She has lost weight and she is always disoriented. What can I do?" Gertrude asked.

"I know the problem. A female witch has cast a spell on your sister. This witch must be more powerful than any of the other witches. I can't see what she is using in my mirror—she is hiding her face. So, I can't tell you who it is," Kokoya said.

"Can you just help me to heal my sister?" Gertrude asked.

"Because I can't see her or what she is doing, it is hard for me to come up with the medicine. But try these roots and dry leaves here," Kokoya instructed.

"Crush the leaves and burn them; then put some of the ashes in your sister's lotion. Let her use that lotion daily. Put the roots in the water in a bucket. Let the roots absorb the water. Let your sister drink that water daily. I suspect your sister was cursed because of the witch's jealousy. The witch thought that your sister would become more successful in the village than the witch's daughter. Put whatever money you brought me on the white plate by the door before you leave," Kokoya added.

Gertrude was very happy that she had found

medicine for her sister. Gertrude did what she was told by Kokoya. Estella used the herbs according to Gertrude's directions. A few weeks passed with Gertrude administering the herb, but Estella did not get any better. Her health continued to deteriorate.

Dr. Kamashi already knew about Estella's illness. One morning, he came to visit her. He checked Estella's vital signs and noted that her blood pressure was normal but her temperature was above normal. He instructed Gertrude to cook hot soup for Estella and assist her in bathing.

"Have you given her pain and fever medications today?" Dr. Kamashi asked.

"Actually, I have tried all this, Dr. Kamashi, and she is not getting better," Gertrude said.

"Well then, we need to take her to a good hospital in Solwezi. Can we organize this now?" Dr. Kamashi answered somberly.

"Where are Ricardo and Felix?" he added.

"Ricardo is visiting his friends and I don't know where Felix is," Gertrude answered.

"Why you didn't tell me earlier that her condition is getting worse?" Dr. Kamashi said, gravely.

As they were talking, Felix returned home. Upon Felix's arrival, Estella was dying on her bed.

Felix rushed to her bed and gripped his mother's hands. He touched his mother's face. He called: "Mother! Mother! Can you hear me?"

Soon after, Ricardo also returned home. He found Felix and Gertrude crying. He touched Estella gently, and she was only staring above her.

Estella's eyes rolled towards Felix but the rest of her body did not move. Felix's tears were rolling down his face. He smelled death in the room. Felix was scared to admit the truth. His mother—the truly most important person in his life—was dying. He was in shock, trying to deny it.

"What am I going to do without her?" Does she know how much she means to me?" Ricardo and Gertrude just held him, their faces pained.

It was the final ending of Felix's childhood and the beginning of his new life. He thought of every moment he had with his mother. He regretted every moment he was away from her, even the moment when he was away, just before she died.

Estella died that morning. Felix felt a huge weight descend upon his shoulders and a vacuum in his life.

Felix found it more difficult to accept his mother's death than Pedro's. He had already witnessed death in his life. However, he struggled to find the meaning of the double losses in his life.

How can I move on from this? What is the point? he often asked himself. After his mother's death, Felix tried many things to find meaning in his life. Still, life stayed empty for Felix. He had nothing except his mother's memories and stories.

Life at this moment was dark for him. Felix did not see any light; he lost hope, strength and vision. One day, as he was alone walking home from the school, he considered suicide as one possible path. However, he did not do this for many reasons. He still loved nature—seeing bushes pass and birds flying in the air. Also, he wanted to carry on his mother's spirit and people who entrusted him.

Felix loved early mornings in the village; the roosters' noise usually woke him up and the sunrises were beautiful. For Felix, nature was full of surprises. Sometimes, the strong wind would blow fresh, juicy fruit off of big mango and guava trees by the paths he walked. He felt blessed by the work of the wind when he walked to school in the mornings. Sometimes the wind blew dust through the air, and his hair and skin would turn pale-reddish while butterflies of different colours and species would be tumbled along. These experiences were vivid in Felix's mind.

He listened to nature around him, and found comfort in the trees and grass interacting with him. He liked the gentle sizzling sounds coming from the tree branches, leaves and grass. He liked being trapped in that moment. He found the frantic car wiper-like havoc of the vegetation comforting.

In addition to the wind, he often heard birds singing—and some songs held meanings to him. One day he told his uncle about a bird's song he had heard earlier that day while he was in the bush. He believed that the song meant he would receive a visitor that day. And that day friends from another village visited him. He greeted them with no surprise and an open smile.

Felix learned to take time to interact with nature. Sometimes he sought comfort from trees; they provided him with shelter from terrible heat or rain. Since he was a young boy, he had hid under their cover to prevent him from getting soaked by the rains during his foot trips to and from school. In many cases, he would be under a tree with a few other students waiting for the rain to stop. Often he did not know the people he was standing with under the trees, but everyone looked happy to be with each other out, warm and dry.

After Estella's funeral, some people in the village had wanted to adopt Felix. They offered to have Felix

An African Orphan

come to live with them. But Ricardo and Gertrude refused to give Felix away. They continued living with Felix, caring for him and paying for his school. Ricardo and Gertrude farmed. They ate most of the crops they grew. They sold a few extra crops, and any money Ricardo and Gertrude made was used to pay secondary-school tuition fees for Felix.

Tobias Mwandala

CHAPTER 9

IN the village, the neighbours were not as near to Ricardo's house as Estella's neighbours had been in Botswana. Here the houses were scattered and the distance between neighbours' homes was measured in kilometers. Regardless of that distance, people in this village often called on one another. Most people in the village shared one tribe. For that reason, people called one another as family members; for example, some people in the village called Felix *brother*; some people called him *son*. Others called him *young brother*; and some called him *cousin*. Some young children even called Felix *uncle* and so on.

In this village, only a few people went to school. Most families trained their children to be farmers and hunters. Also, most of the families could not afford to send their children to school, especially for secondary-school education, which had high tuition costs. Some families preferred using their money to buy livestock rather than spending it on tuition.

Apart from monetary reasons, there were other

reasons why many people in the village did not send their children to school. Some families believed that sending children to school meant losing them. The majority of families felt that they lost control of their children when the children were in school. They believed that school made children to lose their culture. Most children who attended school became more interested in town life than village life; and as a result many of the children did not want to help their parents to farm.

Education was important for Felix. His mother and uncle had taught him that. After his mother's death, Felix felt lonely. He wanted to make some friends in the village. He assumed that it would not be difficult to make friends there since he was cultured in that village. He thought that many friends would accept him. But a number of families did not feel comfortable with strangers teaching their children about life. This made it hard for Felix to get to know many young people when some families discouraged their boys who were his age to associate with him—a school-taught boy with different ideas.

****

In that same year when his mother died, Felix was finishing grade-nine secondary school, the village experienced a drought. In that year's rainy season, there had not been enough rain to keep the famers' crops alive. Farmers in his village relied almost solely on rain as a source of water for their crops. People did not have many alternatives to survive the drought. They did not have modern equipment, electricity or water systems. The water well in Ricardo's backyard became dry. Felix, Ricardo and Gertrude resumed carrying water from a river every day, which was located few kilometers from their house. Ricardo and Gertrude had to sell their goats and chickens in order to survive. Ricardo hated the idea of selling his goats. He had been struggling to save enough to pay the bride price in order to marry his girlfriend.

"I'm not going to sell all the goats. I will keep four goats. When I find the money, I will also buy two cows so that I can marry Josephine," Ricardo declared.

"Well, if we want Felix to finish his education, we must sell all the livestock," Gertrude argued.

"What about me? I also want to live my life," Ricardo asked.

"You have to make choices here. Who knows if the person you don't want to support now is the person that will support you in the future? They say *'baby carry me, I will also carry you.'* Are you forgetting that, Ricardo?" said Gertrude.

"You can always marry later. Besides, Josephine's parents are charging you too much for the bride's price. There are other women out there whose parents would charge you less. Other fathers might even just charge you one goat—not what Josephine's parents want to charge you: six animals! On top of that, they want you to build a big house for them! Think: is that fair to you and us? All that for just one woman? Do you love Josephine so much that you want to sacrifice your family?" Gertrude shouted, with her eyes flashing.

"I have done a lot for Felix, and I still do," Ricardo yelled, pacing around the yard.

"Do you even know if Josephine is a good

woman?" asked Gertrude, firmly.

"You are my sister; don't talk to me like that. Of course I know Josephine very well. If she was not a good person, why would I want to marry her?" Ricardo said, while putting his hands up in the air.

"Can't you see? Can you just please cook for us? Felix is coming from school now," he added.

"Ricardo, you are not listening to me. Is it because you don't think I can give you good advice? Am I only good to cook for you?" Gertrude asked.

"No, no. I have to think about your advice. You are my great sister. We have gone through a lot together: Angola then, and Zambia now. You cook very good meals too!" Ricardo winked.

Gertrude went into the patio and took ten kilograms of corn seeds in a sac, corn flour and two pots from the patio attic. In the patio, the firewood was already ignited. The firewood was always kept lit all day and night, but she added more wood to it so that she could cook quickly. Most of the time, the three of them ate two meals a day: usually sweet potatoes and groundnuts before noon and nshima (corn flour or cassava flour with fish or meat sauce) in the evening.

She found that the corn flour was not enough to cook a meal for that day. Gertrude told Ricardo to go and grind corn seeds for flour. To do that, people in the village went to the boma to grind their seeds using the communal grain grinder.

"Can Felix take the corn seeds to the grinder? I'm fixing the goat shed. One log to the shed is missing. That is allowing that one frisky young goat to get out at night. I have to fix this right away," Ricardo told Gertrude.

"Has Felix ever taken the corn for grinding at the boma?' Gertrude asked.

"It is easy. All you need is money to go to the grinder. I think now they charge fifty kwacha. But there might be a long line-up at the grinder today," Ricardo said.

Felix arrived back at the house around 2:00 P.M. He took off his school uniform and put the uniform away in the house. He put on his regular casual clothes and sandals. He went to his uncle at the goat shed and asked him if he could help.

"Gertrude would like you to do something. She is in the patio cooking," Ricardo instructed.

Felix walked into the patio and leaned forward to Gertrude and asked: "Hello auntie. Do you want me to do something for you?"

"Yes. Your uncle is busy. Can you go and take the corn seeds for grinding? The grain grinder is in the boma, near the office where you got your national registration number. Here is sixty kwacha. You uncle said they might charge you only fifty kwacha. If they do, please buy salt, cooking oil and some painkiller tablets.

"Are you okay auntie?" Felix asked, curiously.

"Yes, I am. It's just headache—that's all," Gertrude said.

"If you go now, you might be in front of the line at the grinder. You will also find some food cooked when you come back. Thank you," Gertrude added.

Felix took the sac of corn seeds and carried it on his shoulders. It was sunny that day. As he walked to the boma, Felix saw a rabbit crossing the bush trail. Felix recalled his uncle telling him about the significance of seeing rabbits. Felix understood that seeing a rabbit on unusual time meant luck. *I'm lucky today*, Felix told himself. After the two-hour walk, he arrived at the market.

"How much to grind a ten-kilogram sac of corn seeds?" Felix asked a male stranger on his way through the market.

"It's thirty-five kwacha to grind a ten-kilogram bag of corn seeds," the man replied.

"Thank you," Felix said.

"Wait, there is another grinder which is fifty kwacha. I heard that this one grind the seeds better than the thirty-five kwacha one," the stranger said.

A number of women were cooking food for sale at the market. Felix smelled the cooking food. Felix felt his stomach growling. He was also tired and so decided to rest at the market for few minutes.

He went to one kiosk where a woman sold fried pieces of small-round handmade bread and homemade drinks. He purchased two pieces of the bread. He used some of the money he was given by Gertrude. *The bread tastes very sweet*, Felix thought.

Felix wanted to balance that taste with a drink. So, he purchased a cup of non-sugary drink that was made by the woman. The drink was made from fermented corn flour and scented dry-tree branches. Felix chewed pieces of the bread slowly and drank bits of non-sugary drink from the cup.

"This tastes delicious. And goes so good with the drink. Thank you," Felix told the woman.

After Felix rested, he resumed his journey to the grain grinder. He did not finish eating all the bread he bought. He put the leftover pieces of bread in his trousers' pockets and continued to eat them gradually as he walked. Since he had used some of the money to buy food he ate, Felix decided to go to the grain grinder where they ground his corn seeds for thirty-five kwacha.

Before he left the boma, he met a tall and well-built man who was wearing a military-style boots, standing at the edge of the market. This man's name was Mr. Jackson and he was a fishmonger at the market. Sometimes he sold different items as well. Felix's interaction with Mr. Jackson came at a right moment, when Felix was struggling to find a meaning and purpose in his life after his mother's death.

"Hey young man," Mr. Jackson asked, with a strong voice. "Do you have a smoke and matches?"

"No, I don't smoke," Felix said, shaking his head sideways.

Mr. Jackson extended his right hand to Felix and said: "My name is Mr. Jackson. What's your name?"

Felix shook Mr. Jackson's hand firmly and said: "My name is Felix."

"You go to school, right?" Mr. Jackson asked.

"Yes, I'm in secondary school," Felix answered.

"What grade are you in?"

"I'm in grade nine," said Felix.

"Form two! Only three forms remaining until you can go to university," Mr. Jackson said.

He added: "I was in form two as well once. But I never had a chance to finish form five (grade 12). I was a professional boxer. I travelled many places with that, and I fought many opponents. I went to Botswana, Namibia, South Africa and Zaire. I made money. I met prominent people. And I had met many beautiful women. I partied."

"I have seen it all. I had both good and hard times. I developed injuries to my body. I became paralyzed.

I couldn't box anymore. My parents had money. They were willing to sponsor me to finish my form five, but I wanted to play and see the world. Yes, I enjoyed my time, but I regret now. I should have finished my form five. It's too late now. I'm not young anymore. My job now is not as good as I could have had if I had finished my school. So I tell young people: Finish school. It goes fast! Felix, you seem to be a bright boy. I'm sure you will go to the university. Finish university and remember me. Become a president and take care of us. Our world needs young people like you," Mr. Jackson advised.

"And now, I shouldn't keep you any longer. Customers are waiting for me and my fish," Mr. Jackson said.

After this conversation, Felix resumed his walk home. When he arrived at home, he felt very tired from walking and carrying the corn on his shoulders. Also, Mr. Jackson had given him many things to think about that evening. He gave the grinded corn and painkiller tablets to his auntie and went in his room to sleep.

Mr. Jackson's advice definitely gave Felix some comfort while grieving for his mother. It helped Felix to think about his purpose in life and his determination to continue his schooling became stronger than before. He realized that attending secondary school was a special thing many people desired.

Although, he was worried about economical support for his tuition from time to time, Felix became increasingly confident in his chosen path. Sometimes Felix was tempted to quit school and start a business. Other times he engaged spending time at the boma, with young men who did not attend school. However, Felix was not negatively affected by these activities. The advice and support of his aunt and uncle ensured that he continued to work hard on his education and follow the right path.

Felix became a regular churchgoer, after his mother's death. Felix enjoyed songs by the local choir, and found serenity during prayers in the church. Felix prayed for his mother's spirit to rest in peace. At times, Felix felt saddened when the choir sang songs that reminded him of his mother's favourite hymns. He would wish his mother were alive and imagined his mother was singing to him.

Many people who surrounded Felix increased his endurance of life. He was receptive in learning new things from them. When Felix was younger, he was scared of thunder and lightening. But Ricardo would tell Felix not to be afraid of the lightening or thunder.

"If you steal from others, lightening could strike you during rainy seasons; but if you did not do anything wrong, you have nothing to fear from the storm," Ricardo advised.

Tobias Mwandala

CHAPTER 10

IN 1985, in the middle of that year, the fourteen-year-old Felix's determination to achieve grade-twelve education was tested as he prepared for his grade-nine school's mock examinations. But still, Felix managed to pass the exams with excellence. His classmates became aware of him. Girls in his class also wanted to spend time with him regularly. Felix felt more powerful as he became noticeable to his classmates. He wanted to maintain the new status he was in. He also felt more pressure to perform well in school. He did not want to disappoint those who looked up to him. Some teachers considered Felix a brilliant student and a good example for other students.

Felix was not a flamboyant student, however. At his school parades he stood in the middle, and at the end of the queues. In the classroom, he never sat in front of the class, except on occasions when he was invited by his classmates to solve math or science problems. Felix enjoyed helping other students. He felt this added another meaning to his life.

Felix's grade nine national and final examinations

were also being prepared at the end of the school year in December. Felix enjoyed this particular year and developed few school friendships.

****

A female classmate by the name of Veronica became interested in Felix. She wanted to have extra lessons with him. On one Friday, during a class break time, Veronica had a chance to talk with Felix in person.

"Are you not going for break time outside?" Veronica asked Felix.

Felix was still sitting on his classroom desk. He tilted his head and responded quietly: "Hi? What's your name?"

"My name is Veronica? You mean you don't know me, Felix? I'm your classmate. I'm sure you know that part," she said, while standing, leaned her body towards him and moved her long hair with her hand to the back of her head.

Suddenly, Felix answered while scratching his right jaw with his index right finger: "Sorry Veronica, sure, I know you, just absent minded here. I'm just trying to solve a math problem from past-exam papers. I have not solved it yet, and it is giving me a headache."

"You study very hard, it seems. You can't even take a break," Veronica said, while holding a textbook in her right hand.

"No, no, no! Have you not seen those guys who got six points (highest grade point) from their final grade-twelve exams last year? Those are the guys who study hard," Felix answered, bouncing his fingers on his desk.

"Felix, can I study with you after classes?" Veronica asked.

"Which subject?" Felix asked, steepling his fingers together.

"Civics," she said, twisting her hair between her two fingers.

"Why civics? I'm not good at civics. Is that the civics textbook you are holding? Can I take a look?" said Felix.

"Sure, you can, Felix. I have seen you answering all the teacher's questions," said Veronica, with her pupils dilating.

Excitedly, Felix answered, "I just answer the questions because I memorize information from the textbook."

Veronica gazed at Felix and said, "I want to learn also how to memorize the information."

"Okay, where would you like to have extra lessons with me?" Felix asked quickly, with his palms open facing her.

"I have seen you staying behind in the classroom after classes are over, so I assumed that you do that for the purpose of studying, right?" asked Veronica.

"Sure," I do stay behind to study more, said Felix, smiling.

"Is that a 'yes,' I can study with you after classes, Felix?" Veronica asked, breathlessly.

Felix nodded his head and said to Veronica, "Yes, we can study together."

Veronica jumped and patted Felix on his shoulders while he was sitting on his desk and said: "Thank you Felix. Thank you. See you later. Remember to take some time from studies. Lets catch up later, and have a great weekend!"

She waved to Felix and left the classroom for the break time.

****

On the Monday after that weekend, Veronica and Felix embarked on their study proposal. A week later, word started spreading around the school that Felix was hanging out with Veronica. It made most other boys in the school jealousy, as they also wanted that opportunity to date Veronica because she was beautiful, smart, attractive and companionable, and she also came from a respected family in the village. Her father was a medical doctor and many people in the village respected him, and they relied on him for medical care as well.

On another occasion after school, Felix and Veronica were studying together in the classroom. They jerked up and looked over their shoulders when they heard the classroom door opening.

"Oh its just me," said Alex, one of their male classmates.

Felix leaned back in his chair, his hands folded behind his head, "Sure, come in! Why not?" he said, staring at Alex.

"Eehh? So its true?" asked Alex, rubbing his chin with his finger.

"What's true?" asked Felix, sitting up and leaning forward.

"I heard it from the moving wind, but now I have seen it with my own two eyes," said Alex, crossing his arms over his chest.

"Is that why you came to spy on us?" asked Felix

clenching his teeth.

"Oh not at all, I just forgot my book in the desk and I came to pick it up," said Alex, while rubbing his eyes.

"Really?" asked Veronica, peeping into Alex's desk that was next to where they were sitting.

"Then how come I cannot see it?" said Veronica.

"Well I left it in there," said Alex, scratching his neck with his index finger.

"Veronica, excuse me one moment," said Felix, grabbing Alex's hand and walking towards the door.

"What are you doing men?" asked Alex pulling away from Felix's arms.

"Just want to have a guy talk with you," said Felix. Alex stopped walking for a moment and winked at Veronica.

Veronica crossed her arms and legs and looked away.

"Felix you are lucky to have that girl," said Alex.

"No it's not what you think," said Felix.

"You mean you two are not….uhm, you know what I mean now, 'doing it'?" asked Alex.

"No, we are just study buddies, that's all," reassured Felix.

"Well you are lucky, that girl is gorgeous, intelligent and comes from a high-class family," said Alex.

"Just study buddies okay," said Felix, while pushing Alex into a walk motion.

"Go home and fetch your parents water from the river, they are waiting for you," Felix said.

Felix returned to the classroom and closed the door behind him.

"What a brat, Alex?" Veronica told Felix.

"I know, he is," Felix replied, looking down.

"Shall we go now? This is sign that we have studied enough for today," Veronica whispered to Felix's ears.

"Yes, sure. Let's go home," Felix whispered back.

They walked out of the school together. They chatted further about their studies. After half an hour of walking out of the school, they departed from each other, and they went to their respective homes.

****

Felix wanted to help Veronica. He felt sorry for her. She wanted to perform well in classes. Also, Veronica's father wanted her to do well in school so that she could become a medical practitioner. But she wanted to succeed so she could become a teacher.

Veronica wanted Felix to be a special friend of hers. She felt intimately connected to him. She had seen Felix sitting by himself in the classroom. Felix was not a sociable person in the school. He liked to concentrate on his studies. Veronica had a few female friends at the school, but she did not relate closely with them.

After classes, Felix and Veronica remained in the classroom and studied civics. Felix made various efforts to teach Veronica all his techniques of memorizing information, including the use of cards and memorizing main concepts. Veronica's marks improved in civics class and other classes as well. She scored excellent grades during the civics classroom exams. Her father was proud of her. Veronica began to develop more tender feelings for Felix than before.

Felix was aware of Veronica's feelings towards

him, but he ignored them. From his standpoint, he only wanted to help her do well in school.

After two months of studying together, Veronica's affection for Felix grew. She wanted to take things to the next level. Although studies were Felix's first priority, Felix could not deny that his heart had started to give way to Veronica's affections. It was all written in his eyes that he admired and adored her in all ways.

One day, Veronica invited Felix to her parents' house. She wanted to introduce him to her parents.

"Can we go to my parents home today after school?" Veronica asked. "I want my dad to know that you are the one helping me with my studies. Is this okay?" Veronica added.

"Are you sure your dad won't mind?" Felix asked.

"Don't worry. He is a good guy. We only study together. Nothing is between us, right?" she said.

"Yes, only studies," Felix answered, rubbing his eyes.

After classes, Veronica and Felix walked on a bush trail from the school to her home, approximately ten kilometers away. Veronica walked very slowly on the trail. She hoped for Felix to walk closely with her. Felix did not want to walk slowly or to be intimate with Veronica.

"Felix, what do you like about me?" Veronica asked, slumping her shoulders.

"You are a good person," Felix responded.

"I also think that you look like my mom," Felix added, smiling.

"Take that back," said Veronica. "I don't want you to like me for what I remind you of."

"Do you know what I like about you, Felix?"

Veronica asked, while gazing at him.

"No, what?" Felix answered.

"You treat me right. You didn't say no when I asked to study with you," said Veronica.

"I like you," she added.

"Thank you," Felix responded quickly and smiled.

Felix felt very happy that moment. Other than his mother, he never thought a female liked him. He did not know what to say or do at that moment. He became quiet. He felt nervous. He began to think about his mother: he started to imagine things he would be doing if his mother were alive. He questioned his relationship with Veronica: *Am I just filling my void of my mother's love? Do I really love Veronica with all my heart?* Felix thought.

Veronica noticed Felix's quietness. "Felix? Felix! What are you thinking?" she said, loudly.

She did not wait for Felix to answer her question but rather went off in a new direction: "Do you want to walk with me to my parents?" Veronica asked.

"Do you know what people say?" Veronica inquired.

"What?" Felix said, putting his hands in his pockets.

"They say: *You reap what you sow,*" Veronica responded with her tight-lipped smile.

"What do you mean?" Felix asked.

"Well, it is a saying my father told me. He said if I want something I need to work at it. Good things don't come without working at them," Veronica explained.

"Do you think there is some wisdom in that?" She asked.

"I think so. Your dad is wise," Felix answered,

cautiously.

Felix and Veronica arrived at Veronica's home. Veronica's father, Dr. Kamashi was standing on a stool outside hanging his clothes on a hang wire. Dr. Kamashi had a well-built body with about five-feet height.

Felix realized Veronica was a daughter of Dr. Kamashi; however, Felix did not tell Veronica immediately.

"Welcome my son, I have heard a lot of good things about you," he said, offering Felix a stool for him to sit.

"I am honoured Dr. Kamashi," replied Felix, as he sat on the stool outside.

While standing, Dr. Kamashi welcomed Felix and shook his hands and resumed hanging his clothes.

Veronica was still standing very close to Felix. Her eyes widened; she asked Felix: "You know my father?"

"Yes, he has been to my house and has helped my family," Felix whispered, softly.

"Fetch him a drink, Veronica," said Dr. Kamashi.

"How do you know my father?" Veronica asked.

"He was my mother's doctor before she died," Felix stated.

"That's good. You guys go ahead and talk. Felix, do you want something to drink?" Veronica asked, as she walked away from him.

"Yes, some water please," said Felix.

Veronica brought a cup of water to Felix and she went to help her father hanging his clothes on the wire. Dr. Kamashi left Veronica hanging the clothes for him.

Dr. Kamashi took another stool, sat on it near

Felix and started chatting with him.

Veronica finished hanging the clothes, and she went in the house to prepare some roasted cassava and roasted groundnuts (Felix's favourite snacks), hoping that Felix would stay longer at the house with her.

"Be a good boy. Remember what you went through during your initiation ceremony," Dr. Kamashi advised, during their chat.

"Thank you, Dr. Kamashi," Felix responded, while bowing his head facing the ground, a sign of respect when talking with elders.

"She is a beautiful girl, my daughter, isn't she?" Dr. Kamashi said, gazing at Felix.

"Yes sir," Felix answered, politely.

"My daughter is a very special one, as you know. Please keep the good work you are doing with her. She is doing well in school. I allow her to be with you, because you are a good person, Felix; and your family is like mine. So, I trust always when she is at school that she is in good company—with you," Dr. Kamashi discussed.

"Thank you sir. I respect you and your daughter, as well," Felix responded, nervously.

Felix felt that the conversation was getting serious about his relationship with Veronica, so he did not want to stay longer.

"I have to go now," Felix said.

"Now?" Dr. Kamashi asked.

"Yes, I have to do something at home," Felix replied.

"Please stay, I'm sure my daughter is preparing some food for us," Dr. Kamashi offered.

"I'm sorry sir; I wish... But I have to go now;

please tell Veronica that I will see her at school," Felix stated.

"Okay, if you have to go, you have to go; but please don't be a stranger. Visit me sometimes," Dr. Kamashi said.

"Yes, I will," Felix replied.

After the conversation, Felix left the house.

****

Felix realized that Veronica wanted a deep friendship with him. However, he was not sure whether or not Veronica was testing him. Felix had never dealt with romantic feelings in his life before. His guidance counselor from the initiation ceremony had told Felix not to engage in any romantic relationship with any woman before marriage. At times, Felix perceived Veronica as a temptation to him.

According to his cultural lessons, Felix was not supposed to have sexual relationships with a woman before marriage. Doing so would mean disappointing his mother's memory and his uncle. At the same time, he did not want to discourage Veronica's interest in him. For Felix, Veronica was special. He felt appreciated and loved by her. Unconsciously, he started also to love Veronica. She resembled his mother—thoughtful and intelligent. Even so, he did not want to turn away from his studies over the friendship he had with Veronica. Felix continued studying hard without responding to Veronica's feelings outwardly.

Felix spent times by himself in the bush trails. He did not invite Veronica to study with him. He started dodging Veronica during school breaks when he saw her. Felix felt too shy to spend time with Veronica in public. Felix did not want other students or teachers to think of him as her boyfriend. He thought that people at the school would not take him seriously if he had a girlfriend. Felix wanted to maintain his good student status. For Felix, to be a good student was to be a person who did not waste his time on frivolous behavior—like having a girlfriend.

Dr. Kamashi was offered a job in Solwezi, where Veronica enrolled in a different school. She also realized that Felix was not ready to be with her romantically.

Felix had ambivalent feelings about Veronica transferring to another school. He felt that he had lost someone close to him—a person he loved. He thought about Veronica regularly.

"I do not know if I will ever find a person like her again," Felix admitted to his uncle and aunt.

Veronica did not write to him. He did not write to her either. Instead, Felix felt Veronica's absence forced him to focus even harder on his studies.

****

When Veronica left, Felix resumed some of his old habits. He went for long walks in the bush trails and climbed trees after school. He read and studied while he was in the bush. Sometimes he did not go to church on Sundays with Gertrude and Ricardo; instead he went to the school to study.

Felix spent many hours at the school studying. On many occasions, he stayed there late into the night. He wanted to be alone most of the time, even though he constantly felt lonely. His closest acquaintances were his books. Once again, Felix was grieving, only now it was for the loss of Veronica, as well as Estella.

Felix joined a choir group at his local church, but his membership did not last long. He stopped going to the group. Although he liked to sing tenor in the choir, he felt that his involvement with the group took away from his school studies.

Sometimes Felix sang songs by himself, when he was walking, bathing, or before he went to sleep. He felt comforted by his singing. He learned how to play drums. He had seen other people in the village using drums, especially during cultural traditions. Drumming became a solace and a welcome retreat for him.

Economical support for Felix was depleting. Ricardo's livestock had decreased and his uncle had already sold some of his goats and chicken in order to support Felix's schooling. Ricardo did not sell all his livestock because he was still hoping to save enough of the goats for his coveted bride price he had been awaiting for several years. Felix did not know where else to turn for help to pay his school tuition fees.

Unfortunately, Gertrude had limited financial resources as well. As a result, she did not have enough money to support her daughter, Lucy in Solwezi, in paying for her school expenses. Thus, Lucy did not finish grade twelve. Instead she got married there. Gertrude felt guilty that she had failed Lucy by not giving her money for her school tuitions. Gertrude had wanted Lucy to graduate from high school and become a nurse.

Although Felix had predicted that Gertrude would not have money to support him financially, he wanted to try his luck—so he asked her if she could give him money to pay for his tuition fees in school.

****

In early January 1986, after Felix wrote his final grade-nine examinations, the fourteen-year-old Felix came home at night. It was a dark night. Gertrude was in a patio sitting near the fire pit, while leaning and supporting her back to the wall. She had placed a pot of water to boil on the fire pit. She wanted to make a tea drink for herself. She was feeling cold that night. When Felix arrived at home, he went straight to the patio and found Gertrude.

"What's the matter auntie Gertrude?" Felix asked, touching his palms on his thighs, while standing and leaning towards her.

"Nothing is wrong, Felix; it's just that I'm feeling cold tonight," she replied, while shivering.

"I hope it is not malaria, is it?" Felix asked, sitting down, with his eyes widely open.

Gertrude still inclining and supporting her back on the wall discussed: "I hope not. Thank for asking Felix. I should call you 'son' because I consider you as my son; you are as the same age as my daughter Lucy in Solwezi. In fact, I would like you two to connect, when you have time. Even, you can travel to Solwezi and visit her during your school holidays. Us folks are getting older. We are not getting young anymore."

"My son, could you please bring tea bags over there," Gertrude said, pointing to the attic in the patio.

Felix stood up and extended his arm into the attic and found the bags of tealeaves.

Just before he sat down, Gertrude asked: "Please add two bags of tea leaves in the boiling water in the pot on the fire pit. Could you please get a cup and add two teaspoons of sugar and give the cup of tea to me?"

"Sure auntie," Felix said, gently, preparing a hot tea drink for his aunt.

"Here it is," Felix extended a cup of tea to Gertrude.

"Thank you my son," Gertrude responded.

"How are your studies, Felix?" she asked.

"They are going well, but one thing I'm struggling with is paying for my tuition fees. Aunt Gertrude, do you happen to have some money you could lend me to pay tuition fees?" Felix asked, humbly.

Gertrude responded: "My son, I'm sorry I don't have any money. I wish I had, I would have already given it to you. Your uncle, Ricardo talked with me about your tuition fees. It's a lot of money that you have to pay in school these days. When I went to school, we never paid for tuition fees. It was free. I love children to attend school. If I had money, I would sponsor all the children in this village to attend school. I know that many kids in this village are not finishing school because their parents don't have money to support them in school, financially. My daughter did not finish school for the same reasons. I wish she finished school. I wanted her to become a nurse. She got married, instead. It happens; I guess the marriage was an expected alternative to finishing school."

"Auntie, don't worry too much about me because you can get sicker. I will find other means to pay for my school fees," Felix said.

"Is there anything else I can do for you, auntie?" he added.

"No, my son, the tea is good. I'm fine," Gertrude said.

"Please take care of yourself, and have a good rest," Felix replied and went to his room to sleep.

****

Two days after that night, Gertrude discovered that she was infected with malaria. The infection was severe enough that Gertrude developed cerebral malaria. Some of her body parts lost sensation. Felix and Ricardo did not have enough money to send Gertrude to a good hospital in the region. They thought the infection would go away, and Gertrude would feel better again.

Yearly malaria was a normal thing for many people in the village. This was one the reasons that Ricardo and Felix were optimistic Gertrude was going to recover. Felix used some of his money he earned from the holiday jobs to buy over-the-counter malaria medication tablets. That was the common action of many of the people in the village, when their loved ones had malaria.

Unfortunately, the medication did not help Gertrude's condition. The infection was so severe that the tablets were not able to stop it from taking over Gertrude's body. As a result, within two weeks of the infection, Gertrude passed away in Felix's arms.

Felix suffered yet another major loss in his life. He felt helpless and guilty that he had not spent more time with Gertrude, and especially with his mother, before they had both passed away.

Felix did not want to die from the disease. He did not want his uncle to die either. He had learned in school that malaria was caused by mosquito bites. He also learnt that sleeping in mosquito nets and clearing mosquito breeding grounds such as waste-dumps and vast grassy areas prevented mosquito bites.

So, Felix began using mosquito nets. He decided to clean the yard. He cut the grass around his house; he closed the old garbage ditch that was on the house yard. He dug a new garbage ditch, dozens of meters away from the house.

Felix was becoming more independent in his life than ever before, as he was forced to raise more money for his school tuition fees and perform the household duties that Gertrude left behind.

****

Several weeks after Gertrude's death, Felix was still troubled by the losses in his life and wondered about ways to support himself while he went to school.

During this time, on some weekends and school holidays, he went to some people in the village to ask for odd jobs, such as weeding on farms. Some people offered him a little paid work. Felix performed these jobs with difficulty. He did not enjoy the work, but needed the money. Felix was still not successful in raising enough money to pay his school tuition fees, however.

Felix kept venturing out to different avenues to make money for his living expenses. Amazingly, even now, Felix did not lose focus on his studies. However, he did start to spend time with young teenagers who were not enrolled in school. This resulted in Felix playing regularly in the streets at the boma.

One evening, while Felix was in a street playing soccer with his acquaintances, one of them suggested to Felix some ways of making money, like selling bananas at the market and eliminating potholes from the main roads near the boma. Felix liked the idea of eliminating potholes from the roads in the town.

The following day, Felix went with his buddies to the main road near the boma. What Felix did not know about the job was that he was both the employer and the employee. He liked that he managed his time to go to work and to leave work when he wanted. However, he felt that it was hard to get customers that were willing to pay for his services. It was time for Felix to enhance his marketing skills further.

Felix and his buddies had shovels, rakes and wheelbarrows. Using wheelbarrows, they took soil from the ground near the road and placed it on the potholes. They raked and mended potholes with their shovels.

While working on the main road at the boma, Felix and his associates stopped drivers who drove the vehicles on this road. They asked the drivers to pay some money to Felix's group, as a courtesy for maintaining the roads. Some drivers paid. Other drivers did not want to.

"Why should I give you money? I pay taxes. So the government should do this, not you young boys. If I give you the money, you will only use it to buy alcohol," one of the drivers accused Felix.

In rainy seasons, the rain removed the soil from

the potholes that Felix and his colleagues had mended. That was good for Felix's business. Still, Felix did not make much money from this job. All the money they received from the drivers had to be shared among all the group members. In addition, Felix's buddies wanted to spend all the money they received from that job buying clothes, snacks and drinks for parties. But Felix wanted to save money to pay for his school tuition fees.

Felix's associates did not like that Felix was hesitant to spend his money to buy stuff or party. Besides that, they also did not like the fact that Felix was attending school and they were not. As a result, Felix finally gave up his associations with his buddies.

****

In that year, 1986, Felix felt confident that he passed his grade nine school examinations. He felt that he had studied hard. And indeed, in the same year, Felix found out that he had passed the examinations with merit. Most of the important people in Felix's life had passed away. But whenever he was at the school, Felix felt that he belonged there. School was all that was left to him.

Felix saved some money he earned from his part-time jobs. He used the money to pay his school tuition fees. But between grade ten and twelve, Felix suffered another economic blow.

Ricardo also left Felix. Ricardo went to Lubumbashi, Zaire to live with a relative there. Ricardo wanted to start a business. He had given up on his farming. Although he went to Zaire, he wished to go back to Zambezi Village a richer person (financially) than before, and to marry and start a family with his dream wife, Josephine.

So Felix was managing his life by himself. That was not unusual in the village. There were a few young people who lived by themselves. There were also many orphans living independently in the village. Some of them were living with grandparents, and those orphans who did not have close family relatives lived with their neighbours.

****

Months passed, Felix continued to survive his life. One hot day of October 1986, the fifteen-year-old Felix received a letter from Ricardo. Ricardo was still in Zaire. Ricardo had given the letter to his acquaintance he met in Zaire. The acquaintance gave the letter to a driver who was driving from Lubumbashi, Zaire to the boma near the Zambezi Village. The driver left the letter to a charcoal seller at the market at the boma. The seller asked around the market to find out who knew Felix. One of Felix's old business buddies happened to be at the bus station near the market fixing potholes. He took the letter from the seller and brought it to Felix. Felix read the letter while he was sitting under the shade of a tree in the boma.

Dear Felix,

I'm here because I want to make a better life for you and myself. You may think I have abandoned you. I have not. I still think about you and your life. Life is difficult as an adult. You will understand this when you grow up. I'm sure you have already started to understand. I'm sorry that I had to leave the country. I'm here to better myself. I know you will make it in life. Do not forget about what I told you about the importance of finishing school. I might come back to the village soon, although I'm not sure when. But, I know that eventually I will come.

I just wanted to let you know that there are people there that are still your relatives: don't forget your sister-cousin Lucy is married and lives in Solwezi. Dr. Kamashi also lives in Solwezi. He is a good friend of ours; you can call him uncle. Please do not feel stuck or alone. Write or visit these people whenever you want. Family is not always people you are born with, but the people you live with also. I hope you are well.

I live in Lubumbashi. It is very busy in this city. Traders are everywhere. There is money to be made. There's business. If I do well, you'll know. Don't worry about me, though. I love you and take care of yourself very well.

Your uncle,

Ricardo

After reading the letter, Felix knew that his survival could not depend on his uncle any longer. In spite of this, he felt his uncle loved him.

It is time for me to focus on my life. I have been given so much. I can do it, Felix thought. The life ahead of him was challenging. Felix had to be courageous to face that future. All he had been left with were his values, education and echoes of love from others who were gone. These things were enough for Felix to survive—he would come to realize that later in his life.

Many days passed after Ricardo's letter. Felix did not eat food some days. He drank water instead. Felix had a five-litres' plastic container, which he covered with clothing and tied to a mango tree branch, so as to cool the water. He also sprayed water on the clothing of the container to make it cooler. Many people in the village practiced that form of water refrigeration.

Felix usually ate only one small meal in the evenings. Sometimes he went to beg for food from food sellers at the market. A number of times Felix picked up pieces of sugarcane from the ground at the market and ate them. Other times he begged for sugarcane straight from the sugarcane sellers at the market.

One day, he was at the market begging some sugarcane from a seller there. The seller told Felix, standing besides the sugarcanes: "I haven't sold any sugarcanes today, and all you want is for me to give you free ones. I'm sorry I can't give you sugarcanes today. Where is your family by the way?"

Felix turned away from the seller and walked. Felix did not respond verbally to the seller. Instead he walked away and thought deeply about that incident. Felix had never felt so isolated in the village. But it helped to remind himself about his middle name. *I am 'Mukeza'—I will return to normal, and this is who I am.*

The following year (1987), a few months after that incident with the sugarcane seller, Felix took steps to return to normalcy. Felix asked for a school transfer from his headmaster at his school in the village. Felix requested the transfer to a secondary school in Solwezi. Not by coincidence, this is the same school

Veronica attended. In his heart, he hoped to be reunited with Veronica. He also wanted to introduce himself to his cousin, Lucy.

Felix sold the chickens and goats his uncle had left him, and used the money to move to Solwezi. He packed up his clothes and personal belongings, and he went to the bus station. He used a wheelbarrow to transport his luggage, including some cooking utensils and farm equipment, to the bus station. Private vans, trucks and minibuses were the usual transportation methods between Zambezi Village and Solwezi. For Felix, the vans and trucks were cheaper to use than minibuses.

Tobias Mwandala

CHAPTER 11

THE year 1987 was a lucky year for Felix. Felix was sixteen years old in that year. August month of the year was dry and hot; wind was blowing with dust in the air and Felix was feeling warm, as he was standing besides the main road at the station. He wanted to hitchhike to save money. Luckily, a five-passenger green Land-Rover truck stopped for him. A European missionary couple with their child from Scotland was travelling in the truck. The family offered a ride to Felix and he accepted the ride. He felt happy that day, sure that this luck was a good omen for his new life in Solwezi.

Felix heard a voice coming from the truck that stopped besides him: "Where are you going, young man?" a man with blue eyes and long face, wearing a white t-shirt, a *safari hat* (brown round hat), placing his hand on the truck's driver window asked Felix.

"I'm going to Solwezi," Felix said, with his luggage on the ground in front of him.

"We are going there too. We can give you a ride all

the way, if you want," the man offered.

"How much will I pay for the ride?" Felix asked, politely.

Felix heard another voice coming from the truck. He saw a kind-faced woman with blue eyes and a ponytail of blonde hair, who spoke with a sharp voice, leaning her head towards the driver's window: "It's free!"

"Thank you very much," Felix said, opened his eyes widely and smiled.

"Put the stuff you have in the trunk. Do you need help to do that?" the man asked.

"I'm okay," Felix answered, while lifting some of the bags from the ground.

Felix packed his belongings into the trunk of the truck. Nonetheless, the man came out of the vehicle and helped him.

"My name is James, by the way. What is your name?" James asked, extending his right hand to Felix.

"My name is Felix," Felix answered and shook James's hand. They finished loading the luggage in the truck.

"Get in the truck," James said and opened one of the side-passenger-back doors. Felix entered the vehicle and sat on the back seat.

The woman wearing brown sandals and a white dress got out of the vehicle, stood besides the truck's passenger side and said to James: "I can sit in the back, he can sit in the front, if you like?"

"It's okay, he is already sitting," James said.

Before James entered the vehicle, he told Felix: "This is my wife, Jennifer. Isn't she beautiful?"

"Yes, she is! Nice meeting you Jennifer; my name

is Felix" Felix said, smiled and shook Jennifer's hand, while sitting in the truck.

"Thank you Felix. I like your sandals and shorts. Hope you did not roast too much from the sun here. Did you wait too long here?" Jennifer responded, also sitting in the vehicle.

"You are so kind mom. I apologize for the dirt from the dust outside. No, I haven't roasted! I'm used to this kind of weather. It's not too bad. Wait until October—when it is too hot such that I can't even walk barefoot on the ground!" Felix responded, smiling.

With Felix on board, the vehicle resumed its journey to Solwezi.

"What are you doing in Solwezi, if I may ask?" James asked.

"I'm going to school there. I used to live in Zambezi Village, but I have now transferred to Solwezi," Felix answered.

"You didn't like the village?" James asked.

"I liked it. It is just that I was alone there. My only cousin in this country lives in Solwezi," Felix explained.

"What about your parents? Where are they?" Jennifer asked.

"My parents passed away when I was younger. My father died in Botswana and my mother died here in the village," Felix stated.

"Oh, I'm sorry to hear that," Jennifer said, in a soothing voice. "What grade are you?"

"I'm in grade eleven," said Felix.

"What do you want to be when you grow up, Felix?" James asked.

"I would like to become a doctor, if things work

out," Felix said.

"Your parents past away, it must be difficult for you going to school without them. Isn't it?" James asked.

"Yes it is, but it can be done."

"How are you supporting yourself in school?" Jennifer asked, with her eyebrows raised.

"I have been working piecework here and there," Felix reported, hastily.

"James, are you not looking for a helper for yard work?" Jennifer asked her husband.

"Yes, I am! Felix, would you be able to help us with that? We live just near the *boma* of Solwezi. You would be able to continue your schooling, while you help us. We have even a bungalow, which you could live in. Think about it—sleep on it tonight. We'll drop you off at your cousin's today, if you like. This is our address. We will be home tomorrow all day. You can visit us then," James offered.

With an open mouth, dropped jaw and his upper eyelids raised, "What?" Felix responded, with a gentle smile.

"Sure, Felix. You don't have to say yes to us, but think about it, okay?" Jennifer responded, kindly.

Before they reached Solwezi, three hours past on the journey. James enjoyed listening to local drum music when he travelled. So, he put on a music disk in the truck radio machine. They all listened to the music.

"Do you like the music?" James asked Felix, while the music was playing.

"It's cool!" Felix responded, gently shaking his head up and down and looking outside through the window.

Felix did not respond right away about the missionary's invitation to him of staying and working at their house. Felix felt astounded and he could not believe that offer by "very-kind white strangers" (missionaries), he thought—was waiting for him. He had to take some time to digest the offer. After three and half hours on the journey, they arrived in Solwezi.

"J and J," Felix said and smiled. "Thank you very much for your offer, regarding working and staying at your house. I will think about it tonight and I will get back to you with an answer tomorrow. You are very kind people," Felix said, nodding his head and widening his eyes.

"Please just drop me here at the boma. I need to ask someone where my cousin lives," Felix requested.

"Have a good night. We hope to see you tomorrow," James smiled.

"Don't you know the address?" James asked.

"No, not really, but many people at the market would know her. I was told that if I mention the name of my cousin's husband, people would be able to take me to her. Her husband is very well known in this town," Felix disclosed.

"What's his name?" James asked.

"His name is Chibaba," Felix said.

"We don't know that name, sorry," Jennifer said.

"Tomorrow is another day!" James said.

"Okay, nice to meet you," Felix said.

****

The family dropped Felix at the boma. He asked a few people at the market, about Chibaba. One man, who said his name was Mr. Chilwa, knew the name—

Chibaba and offered to take Felix to Lucy on his bike. Mr. Chilwa positioned Felix on the carrier of his bicycle and biked to Lucy's house, which was located ten kilometers from the boma. When Felix arrived, Lucy's husband was not home but out drinking with his buddies at a tavern in Solwezi.

"Hello there," Felix knocked on Lucy's house door.

"Who is this?" Lucy shouted, with wrinkles on her forehead, placing her ears towards the door.

"My name is Felix Munga. I'm your cousin from Botswana. I'm coming from Zambezi Village. I just transferred to Solwezi to complete my secondary education," Felix explained, loudly.

Lucy opened the door, and Felix saw Lucy for the first time. Lucy appeared fairly shorter than Felix. She was slender and muscular. She had kept short-black-curly hair, and she had a round face.

"Really! Welcome, welcome my cousin. Feel at home. Good to see you at last. I have heard a lot about you, my handsome cousin!" Lucy said, smiling and widening her eyes.

"You look younger than I thought Lucy. You are looking great my cousin, as if you are not married," Felix said and laughed.

"I might not live with you, though. I intended to, but something happened today. I was offered a job and a place to stay with a European family I met on the road. The family gave me a free ride from the village to Solwezi. They told me to think about their offer. I'm now thinking that things happen for a reason," Felix contemplated.

"What do you think, Lucy?"

"Cousin, sit down first. I will make a cup of tea,

bread with butter and mango jam. This will be your first *Solwezian snack*!" Lucy said.

"Thank you cousin," Felix said and sat on the couch.

"My husband comes home late. Sometimes he does not come home at all. So, you can sleep in the living room. I'll bring blankets for you to use. Tell me about the Europeans you met," Lucy invited, with her eyebrows raised.

"They were really nice people. They treated me well. And yes, they offered me a place to stay, while I work for them," Felix told her, enthusiastically.

With both her mouth and eyes widely open, she said, "Really! Wow, that's nice." And, she quickly added: "So, what did you say? I hope you said *yes*. So, did they give you money as well? I hear that many of them have money. They come to this country with their own money. When they use up all their money, they go back to Europe to their homes to get more."

"No, they said they have a poultry farm. I'm sure they sell chickens for money. One thing I like about them is that they are down-to-earth: they were not pompous. They took me in their Land-Rover truck and talked to me as if I were their own family relative. In fact, they treated me better than my village buddies I had at home. For that reason, I'm considering going to their home tomorrow. They gave me an address," Felix discussed.

Lucy clapped once, patted Felix's shoulder and gently shook her head sideways and said: "That's a blessing cousin. So, you talked to them in English? Can I go with you? Perhaps they could give me a job as well," Lucy asked.

"Yes, I spoke to them in English. I chose to speak

in English because my English teacher told us to practice English language as much as possible, especially when we are with native English speakers. It's the best way to learn the language and attain English principles. We live in a world where English will become the universal language—my teacher told me," Felix explained.

"Not many people I have seen here are from Europe. Most foreign people I see around here are from China and India," Lucy expressed.

After few minutes of chatting with Lucy, Felix was feeling sleepy and tired. He went to sleep on the couch.

****

The following morning, Felix took his clothes and he went to look for the house of James and Jennifer.

"Good luck, cousin!" Lucy said, yawning, while lying down on her bed, covering herself with a blanket.

"Thank you. Let me find out more about these folks. I will let you know how it goes," Felix responded, walking outside the house, wearing black pants, black shoes and a white a shirt, as he wanted to look presentable to the missionaries. He left the farm equipment and cooking utensils at Lucy's home.

The missionary's house was not too far from the town, as James indicated earlier. When Felix arrived at James' house, he saw James walking his dog towards the house; James was wearing a casual safari suit, brown shorts and a brown short-sleeved shirt and brown boots.

As soon as James saw Felix, he lifted his both

hands, palms facing up and called out, "Look who's here! Felix come on in."

The dog started barking at Felix. Staring at the dog, Felix stopped walking towards the house. He was scared. He had never been around dogs before in his life. According to Felix's experience, dogs were kept at home for security purposes, not as pets.

"Keep coming Felix; the dog is friendly. He doesn't bite," James shouted, while walking.

Felix resumed his walk slowly. The house yard was fenced with barbed wire and it had a small gate. The house was made of cemented red bricks. It had a chimney and a poultry house. The distance between the gate and the main house was five hundred meters. Felix, James and the dog walked together to the house. Felix was getting used to the dog. Once inside, James called Jennifer to come and see Felix and to prepare breakfast for him. Jennifer was already in the kitchen cooking breakfast.

Jennifer was walking out of the room, coming to the veranda area in the house, and she was wearing shorts, a white t-shirt and yellow apron, drying her palms with a towel and shaking her head gently; she said, "Welcome come dear friend, Felix. You remembered and located us. Good for you. Please take a seat in the kitchen. I was just preparing some breakfast. You came on a right time. Feel free at home, and James please show Felix whereabouts in this house and may be his to be bedroom outside when you are finished breakfast.

"Thank you," Felix answered, head facing up and gazing his eyes towards the roof.

"Yes, dear," James answered at the same time, also.

Felix sat in the kitchen with James waiting for the breakfast. Jennifer prepared the food. She sat and ate breakfast with them. Felix had never had wheat cereals, yogurt and cheese in his life—all of which he was offered for breakfast. Felix ate the food, even though he did not know how it would taste. He enjoyed the taste and ate everything that Jennifer offered him.

While eating breakfast, Jennifer asked Felix, "So, have you decided that you gonna live with us?"

"Yes madam," Felix replied, with a soft voice.

After he finished, James took him around the house and showed him pictures, including a portrait of James' family, picture of James hunting wild life and a picture of James standing with a president of Zambia.

After the house tour, James took Felix outside and showed him the poultry house, where James' family kept the chicken and their eggs.

"Where do you sell the chicken?" Felix asked, his right hand touching the wall of the poultry.

"We sell them locally. People around Solwezi come to our farm to buy our chickens. Sometimes, we take the chicken into town to sell at the market," James explained.

"Come here Felix, let me show you where we captured the snake: it was bothering the chicken—and us of course. Here is the hole where it lived. We finally killed it after a whole world of trouble. I will show you the skin. I kept it as a souvenir," James chatted, winkling his left eye.

"Usually snakes are okay if you don't disturb them. I learned in the village that snakes bite when you follow them. In fact, one snake bit me on the village farm when I was weeding. I must have disturbed it somehow. I was quite young," Felix chatted back, with his hands in his pocket.

"Jennifer does not like to see any snakes at all. She tells me that I have to get rid of all of them. Perhaps you can help me to do that. Ha-ha-ha!" James smiled and laughed.

Jennifer came out of the house and showed Felix the bungalow that would be his new home. Felix was surprised to see the water-geyser appliance attached to the outside wall of the house.

"What is that?" Felix asked while pointing to the geyser.

"It heats the water that we use for bathing and cooking," Jennifer explained.

"Cool!" Felix said, his eyebrows raised and gently shaking his head up and down.

James and his wife wanted Felix to be part of their family. Jennifer and James did not treat Felix as a houseboy, but as their son. During dinnertimes, the family asked Felix many questions about his hobbies, interests and future goals. They also chatted about life in general.

During the first dinner with the family, Felix was introduced to a Scottish coffee drink that was mixed with sugar and milk powder. Felix accepted the drink.

"Do you drink coffee?" James asked.

"I do on special occasions like this. But I wouldn't call myself a regular coffee drinker," Felix answered.

"Perhaps you are a regular tea drinker, I suspect," James said, glancing at Felix.

"True," Felix replied, politely.

Felix also learned about Scottish table manners. At the table, Jennifer gave Felix a folk, knife and spoon wrapped in a napkin. Felix observed how James used the napkin and utensils. Felix quickly learned about the use of napkin cloth and covered his laps while he ate the dinner. This was the first time Felix had used such utensils to eat. He usually used his hands to eat local food.

Before Felix's mother died, she told Felix to use a fork and knife when eating rice and meat, not nshima. He understood from his mother that a knife has to be held in his right hand and a folk in his left.

"Are you okay using the utensils? You can use your hands if you wish," James said.

"Yes, I'm okay," Felix answered.

"We use our hands when eating *nshima* because then food is part of us. When we use our hands we feel connected with the food. Also, we sit down when eating so as to connect ourselves to the earth and the food," Felix explained.

"Interesting!" James exclaimed.

"Have you found ways to pay for your college studies?" Jennifer asked.

"I don't know. I'm hoping to save all the money I earn from my work here and other places," Felix answered, glancing at both James and Jennifer.

"Good for you! You really want to finish school, yes?" Jennifer said.

"When I came to this country, many things were free, healthcare and education. In fact it is much the same now. I believe you can study at the university here by means of a government bursary. However, in order to get that bursary, you have to score high marks on your final grade-twelve national examinations. This country is rich in natural resources, and its people are very nice. They have been good to us," James stated.

"What do you do here?" Felix asked.

"We came here as missionaries from Scotland. We have discovered that evangelism is much more needed where we came from. Most people here already have faith. Amazingly, dozens of tribes live together here in peace. We have learned to be humble. Even though we were sent here to preach the word of God to the local people, the people are teaching us about the real words of God: *compassion, kindness, peace and love between one another.* We have seen all of that in all the provinces of in this country," Jennifer discussed.

"I want to become a metallurgical engineer so that I can help the country's mining industry. My mother wanted me to become a doctor; but privately, I loved forestry and mining. She didn't want me to become a labourer, but a doctor, lawyer or a politician. I wasn't passionate about those careers when I was young. When I told her that I liked to work in the mine, she agreed only on the condition that I became a director or manager of the mine. I love that this country is the biggest producer of copper in the world," Felix said.

"Yes it is. But, sometimes I feel frustrated about what colonialism did to this country. The price of the copper from here is determined in the UK. Can you imagine that is happening today? I see no sense in that," James stated, clenching his teeth.

"No, I didn't know that. Is it true? Why is that?" Felix asked, tightening his eyes.

"Politics sometimes is complicated. We prefer not to get involved or think about that. We try to remind ourselves that we are here to preach the word of God. What if that means fighting injustice for the poor?"

James discussed.

He added, "Though I'm glad that social developments are advancing here and there. What many people may not know is that blue-collar jobs are powerhouses when it comes to building a country. Although some people may look down upon these jobs, they are much needed, especially when building and developing infrastructure such as rail lines, airports, roads, schools and hospitals. This country has no seaport. It is a landlocked country surrounded by other countries. Generally, it has to use roads or railways to transport its goods abroad."

****

While Felix stayed with James' family, James introduced Felix to western literature, including Germany and French history. Felix learned much about James' family and they about his. Sometimes, James drove Felix to class at his secondary school. James also began to teach Felix how to drive the vehicle. Jennifer too taught Felix how to cook Scottish dishes, including Scotch broth and scones.

Felix learned that the family he was staying with loved him and did not expect too much of him. Although the family was paying him allowances for the work he did at the house, Felix decided not to accept the money from the family. Instead, he told James and Jennifer that what they gave him was enough—a place to sleep and a meaning in his life.

Felix showed his gratitude by working hard on the poultry. He had previous experience raising chicken on the farm in the village. With Felix's work at his new home, James sold and raised more chickens than before. Felix cleaned the yard, cut the grass and loaded chickens into the van for sale. Later, the family gave Felix a van to use for transportation of chicken to the market. He was a faithful and dedicated worker, and James and Jennifer loved him as a son.

****

One day, during his first month at the new school in Solwezi, Felix was at school and bumped into Veronica. Veronica was having lunch with her schoolmates at the school food store.

"Hey, Veronica. It's me, Felix," Felix said.

Veronica's heart *'stopped'* pumping: "Are you the Felix from all those years ago?" she asked, as she rose up from her seat and jumped into Felix's arms.

"I have missed you so much!" cried Veronica.

"It's he, that you know," said Felix, opening his arms wide and scooping her into a passionate tight hug.

"Are you married, any children or girlfriend?" asked Veronica, peering into Felix's eyes, her eyes widened and she was eager for an answer.

"No, I am as single as a *'pole'*," joked Felix, releasing Veronica from the tight grip.

"I met this girl when we were in primary school and ever since then, she never left my mind," said Felix, to the other people that were seated beside Veronica.

"We don't blame you, she is a beautiful girl," they said, laughing.

"Have you never fallen for another girl?" asked one curious guy at a next table.

"I had other petty relationships but Veronica's

face was always in my thoughts, not in a clingy way though," confessed Felix.

"You are that one person on this earth who can actually make me think that the fairy tale of happily ever after is possible," said Veronica, wiping her tears away.

"Where are you staying?" she asked, inquisitively.

"I live with a Scottish family in Solwezi estates," Felix said.

"That's great. We should catch up. Girls, this is Felix my friend from Zambezi Village," Veronica expressed.

"Hi girls?" Felix said, waving his hand at the girls.

"For sure, we should catch up soon. May be I can introduce you to my new family," Felix told Veronica.

"Yes, yes," Veronica said.

"See you soon. Great to bump in you," Felix smiled and started walking away.

"Hey Veronica, how do you know that guy? He looks cool! He looks rich too," one of Veronica's schoolmates commented.

"Do you like him? I'm sorry he is mine. He is taken!" Veronica told the schoolmate.

"Let's go back to the classroom. Lunchtime is going to be over soon," Veronica said, walking back to her classroom and waved her hand at Felix.

Felix purchased a soft drink at the food store. He felt happy meeting Veronica.

"*It is God's plan,*" he told himself.

Felix did not have many friends at the school. Veronica was the only close friend he had. After the encounter, Veronica and Felix met during school breaks and after classes. Their friendship became strong again. Felix took Veronica to his home and introduced her to James and his family. Sometimes, Felix and Veronica went on weekend retreats to Chingola (a town in Copperbelt Province, South of Solwezi). Both of them had fun. They reconnected. Felix thought the relationship was getting serious and he liked it that way. He thought that he was ready to strengthen the relationship deeper.

However, Felix still had a mission in his mind: regardless if anything serious was to happen between Veronica and himself or not, Felix had to finish college. Felix thought that the only way he could pay back his mother was to go to college and become, as she would say, 'someone.' Felix felt that turning away from that goal would be to disrespect his mother's spirit. He remembered his mother's message to him: he had to finish university studies before marriage.

Felix excelled in science and math. In chemistry, he understood intuitively the names and positions of elements on the *Periodic Table* and how to solve chemical equations. He loved biology class, as well as solving matrices, calculus, algebra and trigonometry. This was one of the reasons he continued to consider studying medicine. Nonetheless, the pressure to study medicine came from his mother.

Felix's goal was to study medicine. Veronica wanted to study nursing at a local college in Solwezi. Veronica did not want to talk with Felix about her decision to stay and study in Solwezi, after she completed her high school diploma. She did not want Felix to think that she was running away from him again. Still, Felix continued to be busy with schooling and farming.

Felix did not have enough time to spend with Veronica. She began seeking attention from other boys who visited the school during the school breaks. The boys were not students but worked in the town of Solwezi.

Once again, Felix felt unwanted by Veronica. He stopped communicating with her regularly. Felix felt he had to go somewhere so as to refocus on his life—his studies and career goals. A year after, Felix went to study at a college in Lusaka, after finishing his grade-twelve education.

****

In 1988, after Felix wrote his grade twelve examinations, James and his family had to leave Solwezi. James and Jennifer were assigned to do missionary work in South Africa. The family left their home and farm to Felix.

"You can take care of the poultry and the house. You can build your life here. We love this place but we have to go," James told Felix.

"Here is the address where we are going. Feel free to write us. I'm sure we will be visiting here again. So take care of our house, Land Rover and the snakes!" James laughed.

With tears in her eyes, Jennifer hugged Felix and told him: "Take care. Be safe. We will always miss you."

Felix also felt very sad. He thought about his past and all the people he had missed in his life.

All of my family have left me, Felix thought. Felix said his goodbyes to the family, and the family left that year.

Felix was waiting for his final grade-twelve national examination results. These two moments clearly changed Felix's life. Once again, he felt that he had to choose between his studies and taking care of the house and the farm. He had the potential to earn good money from the poultry farm and live a better life than before. He did not want to disappoint the people who had helped in his life. But he also felt that he owed it to all his loved ones in his past to finish college studies.

In the following year, Felix received his grade twelve examination results. Once again, he had passed the examinations with excellence. Due to the good marks he received from the examinations, Felix won a government bursary to study medicine at a college in Lusaka.

Felix still felt overwhelmed with the decisions he had to make. He understood that he did not have to make the decisions quickly. He felt that he needed an external insight about the matters. So Felix went to Lucy about his new changes in his life.

"James and Jennifer left Solwezi. They went to South Africa. I'm now living at the house by myself. I have been selected to study at a college in Lusaka. What should I do, stay or go?" Felix asked.

"Let's just live together in that big house and raise and sell chickens," Lucy suggested.

"What about all that I have lived for and promised—to finish my college and become a doctor?" Felix inquired.

"Doctors are suffering, Felix. They don't have much money," Lucy said.

"You won't be getting a lot of money from that career, and you know it. Unless that's your passion, you shouldn't do it," Lucy advised.

"Of course I wouldn't do it only for the money. I

think I like medicine," Felix said.

"Can you live in the house while I go to Lusaka and study?" he asked.

"Sure, I can ask my husband if he would accept. I see no reason why he would refuse. He only comes home at night, anyway," Lucy sighed.

"Have you talked to your in-law parents or elders in your community about this problem?" Felix inquired.

"Yes, I have talked to his parents; they told me that I should give him some time to change. But they also said we should resolve the issue ourselves. I felt that they were suggesting that there's something that my husband is not getting from me; and that's why he always hanging out with his buddies everyday and he comes home late," Lucy explained angrily.

"Do you know any man that you trust? May be you can talk to him so that he can talk to your husband," Felix asked.

"You," Lucy laughed and pointed her index finger at Felix.

"Well, yes, but I'm not older than your husband, so he wouldn't listen to me. I wish I were older than he. I would help you in that way," Felix stated.

"I know one elder in my community. I will talk to that elder and see what will happen," Lucy said.

"Let me know, regardless. I will be going to Lusaka when the school term starts this fall," Felix said.

As a young man, the eighteen-year-old Felix had never been to a big city like Lusaka. When he arrived, he was surprised to see modern facilities such as big buildings, supermarkets and monuments. He did not feel that he belonged to the city. Instead, he thought that his lifestyle and mannerisms fitted in the village.

At the college he spent most of time alone studying. There were many students from different places, including other countries. Felix lived in the college hostels, where he spent most of his time after class. He cooked for himself and sometimes ate lunch in the college cafeteria. Felix found the college environment very competitive. Every year, Felix had to pass exams to proceed to a next level of his studies. Failing an exam meant repeating a year of studies.

In his second year, Felix had an awakening. He was no longer interested in medicine as a career but agriculture. He felt wholeheartedly that he needed to help people in the village grow more food. When he realized that the knowledge of farming was much needed where he came from, Felix switched from the medical program to an agriculture program within the same college.

The program length was shorter than the medical program. He was left with only two years to complete the program in agriculture. During the college holidays, Felix did not go to his home in Solwezi. He wanted to gain more knowledge of farming on a variety of crops. Thus, he spent his holidays working for private farmers in Kafue district, near the college. While Felix was in his third year of the program, he received two letters. One came from Veronica and another from his cousin Lucy.

Lucy wrote:

Dear Felix,

> Thank you for the place you left us. My husband agreed to move to the bigger house. I also talked to an elder about my husband. My husband has

changed. He no longer comes home late. I'm not sure what caused the change. I really don't know how that happened. It could be because of the house we are living in now. It's nice and big and everything we needed when we got married is here: big yard and farm equipment, and inside the house is everything we never had before. My husband has taken an interest in farming and he seems to be doing well with that. When you come, you will see what has happened to him. He is a changed man. I'm happy for him and for us. It may be because of this or because the elder talked to him and he listened. I don't know. All is well here. I hope your studies are going okay. We need a doctor in our family. Please come back when you finish schooling.

Write back,
Lucy.

Veronica wrote:

Hello Felix,

How are you? I hope your studies are going well. Mine are almost done. I don't know what to say. I feel that I did something wrong to you. I know you want to be away from this life. Are you coming back to Solwezi? I heard that you are studying medicine. You know that I want to become a nurse here. Do you want to work in Lusaka? Or are you going to South Africa? Let me know how you feel about me. I want to know. I'm sure you know how I feel about you. I'm sorry that I didn't communicate this earlier, when you were here. Perhaps, I wasn't ready.

I have seen my friends go to other places but Solwezi's population has increased. There are new people coming and many foreigners as well. They are building roads and companies. It is not like the way you left it. The place has changed. I still love Solwezi, and I want to work here as a nurse. By the way, my father asked me about you and he said I should pass his warm greetings and blessings to you.

Please let me hear from you.

Missing you,
Veronica.

Felix wrote a back to Veronica:

Dear Veronica,
Thank you for your letter. I'm very happy to hear from you. I'm finishing school here soon and I'm coming back to Solwezi next year. I can't wait to see you there and catch up with everything. I miss you so much as well. Felix.

He also wrote back to Lucy:

Hi Cousin,
I'm very happy to hear from you and to hear that things with the farm and your husband are going well. I should be finishing soon here and I will return home next year for sure. About medicine, I switched this to another program, but long story short—I'm happy. We'll talk more later. We have exams shortly and I have been studying a lot for them.
Please take care and keep up your magic you are doing with your hubby!
Your cousin,
Felix.

****

In 1993, the twenty-two-year old Felix completed his program and graduated with a degree in agriculture science. Felix was very happy.

The following day after graduation, he took a bus back to Solwezi. When he arrived at his house, he found the poultry farm and a large garden of vegetables tomatoes, onion, cabbage and lettuce thriving.

In addition, Lucy and her husband had kept the money they received from selling chicken and vegetables. Lucy showed the money to Felix. Felix's idea of helping farmers developed.

Felix, Lucy and her husband began living together. Felix continued to sleep in the bungalow and Lucy and her husband slept in the main house.

One day, Felix went to the local government (located at the boma in Solwezi) to propose his big plan. Felix's plan was to start a farming school to teach peasant farmers in the community about effective ways of farming, including poly-culture farming and irrigation-farming methods. The local government staff advised Felix to talk to elders in the community and ask their opinion regarding the plan.

So Felix had a meeting with the twelve elders of the community to discuss his plan with them. Elders told him that he meant well, but that they wanted him to first pay respect to the gods of the community by donating any money he had to buy ceremonial wine and food for them before he proceeded with the plan. Felix did as he was advised.

After one week, he went to the boma and received the permit from the local government people for his plan to build a farming school.

With the help of donations of labour, building

materials, machinery and money from people in the community, Felix built a school that could accommodate fifty people. Felix hired volunteers in the village to teach the farmers. The project was called *Brothers and Sisters Farming Together*. Farmers went to each other's farm to learn and work together. They rotated from one farm to another—with the goal of helping each other and bettering existing farming methods. Felix would visit each of those farms and offer his leadership and knowledge regarding farming.

Felix felt fulfilled in his life. He was happy that he had finally found something that was important to him and helped the people in the community that had supported him in his turbulent life.

Veronica's father, Dr. Kamashi had also joined the project, as a researcher. One day, Dr. Kamashi invited Felix for a cold soft drink meeting at the market, at the boma. While they were chatting about the project and drinking their soft drinks, Dr. Kamashi grabbed Felix's hand and looked at Felix, in his eyes, Dr Kamashi asked: "Have you talked to my daughter recently? What does she think about you leading this farming project?"

"I have been very busy, sir. But I plan to be meeting with her very soon," Felix answered, quickly.

"I am glad you have joined this project, Dr. Kamashi," added Felix, nervously.

"I am sure this project will benefit from your expertise as an experienced elder," added Felix.

"Don't ever forget that," joked Dr. Kamashi.

"Talking of wisdom, I have some words of wisdom, I would like to share with you," he added.

"Come closer my son," he said, beckoning Felix

with his hand.

Felix pulled his seat closer to Dr. Kamashi's seat.

"You know our elders have a saying that elders have more wisdom than youngsters?" Dr. Kamashi asked.

"Yes sir," said Felix, removing his cap from his head and bowing his head as a sign of respect to an elder.

"As you have achieved your dream of starting your project in Solwezi, your next goal should be to settle down and start a small family of your own," Dr. Kamashi said.

"As you, may already know, a man's strength is in bearing children to succeed him; without a son, a man has no reason to wake up and sweat from working under the sun," he added clearing his throat.

****

A week later, Felix asked Veronica to take him to meet her parents. Veronica's mother was very excited and passed word across to all her family and friends.

"My daughter has found a man, my soul rejoices, come and celebrate with me," she announced.

Felix arrived with a small gift (African fabric/scarf) for Veronica's mother and a small gift (Kola nuts) that he and Dr. Kamashi could share on the porch at his house.

"You do know that at some point, as a dad to my little girl daughter, I do worry about letting go of my little girl?" asked Dr. Kamashi.

"You can depend on me to take care of her when you do let go of her," responded Felix.

An African Orphan

Tobias Mwandala

CPSIA information can be obtained at www.ICGtesting.com
Printed in the USA
LVOW06s2008220414

382766LV00001B/7/P

Acknowledgement

I thank people I have met around the world, support, kindness, love and openness. I'm very my father who has a huge heart for orphans. great inspiration. I'm grateful also to my editor great help.